BETROTHED
— TO THE —
PRINCE

RAYE MORGAN

SILHOUETTE *Romance* ®

Published by Silhouette Books

America's Publisher of Contemporary Romance

To Jean, for all the days of laughter.

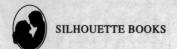 **SILHOUETTE BOOKS**

ISBN 0-373-19667-9

BETROTHED TO THE PRINCE

Visit Silhouette at www.eHarlequin.com

Printed in U.S.A.

Books by Raye Morgan

Silhouette Romance

Roses Never Fade #427
Promoted—to Wife! #1451
The Boss's Baby Mistake #1499
Working Overtime #1548
She's Having My Baby! #1571
A Little Moonlighting #1595
†*Jack and the Princess* #1655
†*Betrothed to the Prince* #1667

Silhouette Books

Wanted: Mother
"The Baby Invasion"

†*Royal Nights*

Silhouette Desire

Embers of the Sun #52
Summer Wind #101
Crystal Blue Horizon #141
A Lucky Streak #393
Husband for Hire #434
Too Many Babies #543
Ladies' Man #562
In a Marrying Mood #623
Baby Aboard #673
Almost a Bride #717
The Bachelor #768
Caution: Charm at Work #807
Yesterday's Outlaw #836
The Daddy Due Date #843
Babies on the Doorstep #886
Sorry, the Bride Has Escaped #892
*Baby Dreams #997
*A Gift for Baby #1010
*Babies by the Busload #1022
*Instant Dad #1040
Wife by Contract #1100
The Hand-Picked Bride #1119
Secret Dad #1199

†Catching the Crown
*The Baby Shower

RAYE MORGAN

has spent almost two decades, while writing over fifty novels, searching for the answer to that elusive question: Just what is that special magic that happens when a man and a woman fall in love? Every time she thinks she has the answer, a new wrinkle pops up, necessitating another book! Meanwhile, after living in Holland, Guam, Japan and Washington, D.C., she currently makes her home in Southern California with her husband and two of her four boys.

THE NABOTAVIAN ROYAL FAMILY

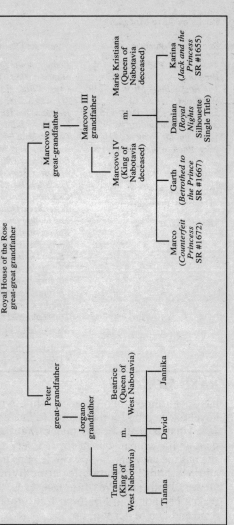

Chapter One

"Hello. What have we here?"

Princess Katianna Mirishevsky Roseanova-Krimorova, usually known as Tianna Rose, stood looking down at the man sprawled on the cushioned gazebo bench with a reluctant sense of interest. It was pretty obvious he was sleeping off the effects of a night on the town. She couldn't imagine how the staff who administered to this royal residence could let such things go on.

"Shoddy maintenance," her mother would have said. This certainly wouldn't have been tolerated at her parents' home.

But this casual attitude seemed to be common here on the Arizona estate of the Roseanova family—the home of the exiled Royal House of the Rose. She'd arrived at the address, dismissed her cab and gone to the entry gatehouse, only to find the gate standing wide open and no one in attendance. The estate where she'd grown up was much more modest and low-key than this one, and yet such lax security was unheard of there. And besides that, she'd assumed there would be a shuttle service to take her to the main house, and now it looked like she was going to have to make the uphill climb on her own.

Sighing, she started up the long driveway, only to notice the cute little gazebo overlooking a small man-made lake. She could see someone was inside so she made the detour in hopes of finding help. But it seemed she was destined to be out of luck again. The man was out like a light.

Still, he was so good-looking, even in this state, that she lingered, looking him over for a moment. He looked quite comfortable lying on a sort of window seat setup equipped with plush cushions. His dark blond hair was tousled and a little too long, but his white shirt, though partially unbuttoned, was impeccable, his leather jacket expensive-looking and his slacks still had a beautiful crease. His features were strong and even, his skin smooth and tan. The slight stubble on his chin only enhanced the effect of very appealing masculinity. All in all, he was gorgeous. They just didn't hire them like this where she came from—more the pity.

She thought about giving him a quick shake and waking him. But no. That wouldn't be much use. She might as well get back on the path and make her way to the main house. Pulling her wine-colored suede jacket a little closer in the cool fall morning air, she gave one last glance at the muscular exposure of his impressive chest and turned to go. To her horror, his hand shot out and grabbed her wrist, trapping her.

"Hey, Little Red Riding Hood," he said in a voice low as a scratchy old cello. "Didn't anyone tell you it isn't safe to wander around alone in these woods?"

"Let me go!" she ordered once she found his grasp was like steel.

"Oh." His eyes were barely slit open. "Sorry. I thought you were part of my dream." But he still held her.

She tugged on his hold, definitely annoyed by now.

"Listen," she began, but he wasn't listening at all.

"You're sexy enough to be part of my dream," he was musing whimsically. "And you'll definitely be a part of my next dream."

"Make that your nightmare," she snapped, reaching to grab his thumb and bend it backward, hard, turning into it to make a clean breakaway.

"Hey!" he said, and swore as he dropped her wrist and began to struggle to sit up. "What the—?"

But she didn't stick around to chat. Head high, she marched toward the driveway without a backward glance, silently thanking her personal defense trainer as she went. So much for those who thought princesses were sitting ducks for any passing tormentor. It was actually rather satisfying to have run across a chance to use her training.

The entire incident was timely. She'd needed a little boost to her self-esteem to help her through the chore she'd set for herself here. She'd come to break her engagement to Garth Franz Josef Mikeavich Romano Roseanova, Prince of Nabotavia. She was going to have to be tough to make him understand that she was not going to marry him, no matter how many official proclamations of their betrothal he could pull out of the country's archives.

Not in a million years.

The inner area of the estate was set off by a long arbor covered with winding sprays of climbing red roses, and she paused at the lovely gateway to gaze in at the spires and towers and balconies decorating the huge palatial mansion ahead, giving a little cough of amusement.

"Just like an East Nabotavian prince to build himself a little Rhineland castle in the middle of Arizona," she thought to herself.

She was a West Nabotavian herself, one of a contingent of refugees who had fled the tiny Central European country twenty years before during a deadly revolution. Most had landed in the United States, living relatively good lives, working and waiting for their chance to rid their country of its oppressors. Now a miracle had happened and the rebels had been thrown off. Nabotavia wanted its monarchy back, and young people such as Tianna were preparing to return to a land they only knew in legends. But it was their home, their destiny. Anyway, it was supposed to be.

Tianna was having trouble reconciling her own plans with this new imperative. She didn't know how Prince Garth felt about it, but she had no intention of going back. And that was one reason she meant to break their engagement off right away.

A scattering of raindrops made a pattern on the walkway and she looked up at the dark clouds gathering above her in the huge Arizona sky. Somewhere not too far off, thunder crackled. Good thing she wasn't too far from the house.

A shout drew her attention. Some sort of a hullabaloo seemed to be going on in another area of the estate. She could hear some yelling, a man's voice, then a woman's higher shriek. Craning her neck, she spotted the location of the activity. Two large cows were munching contentedly in the vegetable garden while a number of people were dancing around them, yelling and waving hats and brooms and other implements of distraction. That solved the mystery of where the security guards must be.

Shrugging lightly, Tianna walked through the arbor and started toward the house, the sensible heels of her soft leather shoes making a pleasing tattoo on the flagstone pavers. But another sound stopped her in her tracks. She turned, frowning, not sure what it was. The soft noise was coming from just beyond the primrose beds that lined the driveway. It seemed to be coming from a small bundle wrapped in a blanket and was certainly something alive. A kitten? A puppy? She moved forward hesitantly and lifted the edge of the little pink blanket.

Her heart stopped. A baby. Big blue eyes stared out at her and the sweet little mouth made a tiny *o*.

"A baby!" she said to no one in particular. "Oh, you precious little thing."

She looked around quickly, sure that someone must be nearby who was in charge of this sweetheart. But there was no one in sight. Perhaps the nanny had stuck the baby here while she ran off to help with the cows. Another inept employee! What a strange place this was—and how glad she was that she wasn't going to be marrying the prince and living here, even temporarily.

But the raindrops were coming harder all the time. Without any more hesitation, she shifted her overnight case to her other hand, reached down and scooped up the baby and headed for the house. She'd been aiming at the front door, but the side entry looked closer and the door there was open, so she changed her trajectory and made a beeline for that.

"Hello!" she called, stepping in out of the drizzle and into the huge kitchen, shaking the drops from her rich copper-colored hair and setting her overnight case by the door.

A teenage girl with a snub nose and a mop of bouncing curls came forward to greet her. "Oh, did you come for the pastry job, then? I think you're a bit early."

"The job?" Tianna looked at her blankly, pressing

the little live bundle to her chest. "Oh, no, actually..." She shook her head and smiled at the girl. "No, I've come to see the prince."

"The prince?" Her dark eyes widened. "Sorry. He's not here."

"Not here?" Tianna said with dismay. She'd had her family secretary call and check and they'd said he would be in all this week. *Oh!* She should have called herself, just to make sure. But she'd assumed the information would be good.

Still, she'd come here on the sly, so what did she expect? Her parents thought she was visiting an old school friend in Phoenix. Instead, she'd slipped over to Flagstaff in order to talk Prince Garth into joining her in annulling their betrothal.

They'd been engaged since they were small children, an arrangement set up in a case of influence swapping that had long since lost its importance, as far as she was concerned. And since he'd never shown the slightest interest in her—they had never even met—she had high hopes she was going to be able to pull it off and present it as a fait accompli to her father.

"Where has he gone?" she asked the maid.

The girl shrugged again. "I don't know. I think maybe Texas."

"Oh no." Tianna couldn't believe she'd come all this way for nothing. "Do you have any idea when he'll be back?"

"No, Miss. I'm sorry. He doesn't come here much lately."

The baby squirmed and made a tiny sound, more like a kitten than a child and Tianna gave it a comforting pat.

The young maid looked confused. "Is that a baby?"

"Oh, yes." Tianna held it out where it could be seen. "Someone left this baby outside in the rain. I thought I'd better bring her in."

The maid blinked. "Outside in the rain?" she echoed blankly.

"Exactly," Tianna said. "It must belong to someone here."

"No, Miss." She was shaking her head quite emphatically. "There's no baby living here. I would know if there was a baby here."

"Oh, for heaven's sake," Tianna murmured, looking down into the precious face and feeling a pang of sympathy for the poor little thing. All alone, with no one to claim her. Something tugged at her heart as she remembered another little girl lost from her own past. Wincing, she hugged the baby to her heart and murmured a comforting sound.

"Cook's not here," the little maid went on. "They're all out chasing the cows. They got out again and went straight for the vegetable garden, like they do every time." She gestured toward a chair. "Please sit and wait, Miss. Cook will be back in no time. I'll go fetch her and tell her you are here for the pastry job."

The girl bobbed her head and before Tianna could

correct her again, she disappeared down a dark passageway.

"Oh!" Tianna looked down at the tiny life in her arms and her annoyance melted. "You are so beautiful," she whispered, kissing the downy head. "But what am I going to do with you?"

She looked around the room for a place to put the baby down, but though the huge kitchen managed to have a homey ambience, with copper-bottomed pans displayed over a central island and swags of herbs hanging in a window, its shining stainless steel counters and appliances didn't seem to have a niche for a baby to sleep in.

Someone was coming down the hall toward the kitchen and she turned, hoping to find an adult who could be talked to instead of the witless little maid. There was a muted groan before the newcomer appeared, a hand held to his head, his eyes barely slit open enough to make his way.

Tianna gasped. It was the reprobate who'd been lolling about in the gazebo. She stood where she was, paralyzed. A woman who prided herself on her levelheaded attitude toward life, she was not one to be bowled over by a handsome hunk, but this was, without a doubt, the most stunning man she'd ever seen, and now that he was upright, he looked even better than he had a few minutes earlier.

Her trained photographer's eye told her she was looking at a masterpiece. His physical beauty shone through despite the fact that his golden hair needed cutting and he'd changed his clothes into something more casual. Dressed in a pair of snug jeans and a cotton shirt left carelessly open to display that breathtakingly muscular chest, he was absolutely spectacular in a young-god-straddling-the-universe sort of way. She might have taken him for the prince himself if she hadn't already heard the prince was gone.

But no. The few princes she'd met over the years had mostly been effete and purposeless, dried husks of the men of power they might once have been. This man was too earthy, too vital, to be a prince. He looked more like a warrior. A warrior who'd had too much to drink recently.

"Haven't we met somewhere?" he asked, gazing at her through narrowed eyes, as though the room was too bright for him.

"You might say that," she said crisply, determined he wouldn't know how attractive she found him. "You could be having trouble remembering, since you were lying down at the time."

"Oh yes. The girl of my dreams." His crooked smile was a knock-out, but it was fleeting. In seconds he was putting his hand to his head again and wincing. "Sorry to present myself in such a state of disrepair," he added. "I'm recovering from a rather late night."

"So I see."

"Ouch. Your tone has the definite sting of disapproval." He raised a sardonic eyebrow. " I don't suppose you've ever had a hangover, have you, Red Riding Hood?"

"Never."

"No. I didn't think so. You're one of the wise ones. It's written all over you." He sighed. "I think I've finally learned that lesson myself. I know I'm never going to touch alcohol again." He looked around the kitchen as though he'd lost something. "What do you know about making Bloody Marys?" he added hopefully.

"Nothing."

She made her tone as scornful as possible, but she knew she wasn't fooling anyone. If she'd known a magic potion to make him feel better, she'd have conjured it up in a flash. As it was she just stood there, watching him, holding the baby to her chest. She'd always known pure beauty could be fascinating, but she'd never experienced it in the form of a man before.

He nodded, accepting fate for what it was, and rummaged in a cabinet, finding a remedy for himself. Tearing open a package, he poured the contents into a glass and filled it with water from the faucet in the huge stainless steel sink, then downed most of it, making a face as he set the glass back down on the counter.

"Not quite as satisfying as the hair of the dog," he murmured as he made his way painfully toward the kitchen table. "But probably more effective."

Slumping into a chair, he threw his head back and closed his eyes and wondered, and not for the first time, why he put himself through this sort of punishment. Admittedly, it had been a good long time since he'd tied one on like he had the night before. At one time it had actually seemed like fun. As the years went on, it had become rather dreary, and he'd pretty much given up the party scene. But last night...

He wasn't kidding anyone. He knew why he'd tried to drown himself in a bottle the night before. The anniversary of his parents' murder was a tough thing to get past, and last night had been the twentieth one. Hopefully by next year this time he'd be too busy in Nabotavia to go through this yearly ritual.

He opened his eyes and found himself staring right into the steady green gaze of the young woman gently pacing back and forth in front of him. Suddenly he was almost embarrassed by his condition. She was so young and bright and clean-looking. He felt shopworn and seedy in contrast. He sat up a bit straighter.

"What have you got there?" he asked, noting the bundle she carried close to her chest.

She cuddled it closer, pressing a kiss to the tiny head. "A baby," she replied, gazing at him over the top of the blanket.

Suddenly he was wide-awake. "A baby?" He sat up even straighter as the implications became clear to him. "Your baby?"

"No." She glanced at him, then away again. "Someone left her out in the yard. I just brought her in out of the rain."

"Uh-huh."

That hardly seemed likely. Now he was guarded. He tried to remember if she'd been carrying the baby when he'd first seen her in the gazebo, but he hadn't been thinking clearly enough at the time to notice much of anything. He frowned, focusing. Had he ever seen her before? No, he didn't think so. He would have remembered. And she wasn't claiming any previous relationship at this point.

"I know nothing about babies," he said, as though merely making conversation. "I've heard they have something to do with human beings, in much the same way the acorn magically transforms itself into the mighty oak, but I have a hard time believing it."

She wasn't paying any attention to his jesting declaration. Her face was bent down to the little one and she was murmuring soft sounds to it. He frowned. She did seem inordinately attached to a baby she'd only just met. He couldn't help but be suspicious.

One thing he'd been scrupulously careful about all his adult life was to make sure there would never be a woman who could claim her baby was his. There had been a few who had tried that scam, but the claims had never held up. Still, it had happened often enough to make him very wary.

He'd learned very young that his special station in life meant there weren't many people he could trust. Everybody seemed to want something from him, whether it was influence or favors or just the extra prestige of being able to say they had been hanging out with the prince. He didn't often let his guard down. The few times he'd done that had led to pain and disaster. His carefully maintained image of vaguely good-natured cynicism was real in part, but it also served to hide an inner vulnerability he wouldn't ever risk again.

"So what's it doing here?" he asked.

She looked at him as though she was beginning to doubt his intelligence. "It's a baby," she said carefully.

"But not yours."

"No, I found it in the yard."

"So you said." His mouth turned down at the corners. "So whose is it really?"

She cocked an eyebrow at him. "I don't know, but your gate was unattended. Almost anyone could have sauntered in."

"True." He wasn't convinced, but then, it didn't really matter. He didn't have much interest in babies anyway. But he did like the look of the woman who held it. "So you think things are a little lax around here, do you?"

"That's putting it mildly," she said without bothering to soften her judgment. "This place is run like a public park."

"Oh. I suppose you think you could do a better job."

She gave a short laugh. "I know I could."

He liked her attitude. It was refreshing to meet an attractive woman who didn't seem to be bowled over by just being in his presence. "Really. If you took over management, what would you do to improve it?"

She gave him a sideways look and went back to

rocking the baby in her arms. "My first item of business would probably be to fire *you.*"

"Fire *me?*" He stared at her for a moment, then threw back his head and laughed.

"Absolutely." She followed up her assertion with a scathing glance that went up and down the long, muscular length of him, and was meant to convey disapproval, but ended up feeling too much like admiration for comfort and she quickly looked away. "I would never put up with an employee who acted like you do." She shifted the baby from one hip to the other. "What do you do around here, anyway?"

He grinned. She really didn't know he was the prince of this castle. That was great. "Oh, not a whole heck of a lot. Mostly they just keep me around for comic relief."

"Really?" Her look told him she halfway believed it. "Well you could make yourself useful right now. Would you like to hold the baby for a moment?" She offered the little bundle with the blanket open so that the baby could be seen.

He glanced at it and looked away, shaking his head dismissively. "I'm not much of a baby person."

She stepped toward him. "Hold her anyway, while I fix a place to put her down."

Not likely. Something about the thought of taking charge of that little piece of life gave him the willies. He threw her a baleful look. "*I'll* do it," he said, rising and looking around the kitchen, grabbing a large basket and arranging the napkins it held into a sort of bed. "Here you go."

She carefully laid the sleeping child in the impromptu bed and pushed it to a safe place on the counter, then looked down with a sweet smile. "She's so beautiful."

He'd never considered red and wrinkled to be beautiful, but he did like the look of the woman. She interested him. She kept looking at him in the oddest way. It wasn't just that she was attracted to him. Women usually were. But there was something more, something mysterious in her smoky green eyes.

She was very pretty, but it was a careless sort of beauty. The way she held herself, the way she moved, he could tell she didn't think about her looks any more than she thought about the weather. There was an innocence about her, and yet at the same time, a sophistication, as though she knew a lot, but it was mostly secondhand information, experience gained from books and not from mixing with the masses.

"Funny," he said softly, looking at the way her bronze hair lay against the smooth pale skin of her neck and wondering if she smelled as good as she looked. "You don't look like a pastry chef."

"I am not a pastry chef," she responded automatically, looking up at him. It didn't occur to her to say she was a princess. She never said things like that. If she had her way, the whole princess thing would fade from her life and no one would ever know about it again. Of course, being a princess was the very reason she was here, a fact she had practically forgotten by now.

"I saw Milla, the kitchen maid, in the hall and she said you'd come about the pastry chef position."

Tianna gave him a long suffering look. "Milla was wrong."

He frowned. Thinking wasn't as painful as it had been a few minutes earlier, but it still wasn't back with its usual zing. "What are you, then?"

"I'm a photographer."

He groaned, dropping back down into the chair and stretching. "Not another photojournalist sniffing around for a story on the royals."

"I'm not a photojournalist," she assured him quickly. "I told you, I'm a photographer. I mainly concentrate on architectural photography. And I have no interest in photographing royals."

"Good. Then we won't have to kick you out on your ear."

She bristled. "I'd like to see you try," she said sharply, one hand on her hip.

"Oh. That's right. I forgot you were the dangerous one." His blue eyes glinted at her in a way that sent a new awareness skittering along her nerve endings. "Quite the little wild cat, aren't you?" he said in a tone that made her sound downright erotic.

Her breath caught in her throat and color flooded her cheeks, but she lifted her chin and tried to ignore it. "I'm nothing of the sort. But I do know how to defend myself."

"I'll say you do. I've got the sore hand to prove it." He shook the hand, deemed it basically unscathed, but looked up at her accusingly anyway. "That was quite a nice demonstration of the old thumb trick you put on this morning. What other escape moves do you have up your sleeve?"

She looked fully at him and for just a moment, their gazes seemed to connect, fuse, and sizzle.

"I...I think I'd better keep that to myself," she said, feeling a bit muddled and looking toward the window, absently noting that the rain was coming down pretty steadily now. "The element of surprise is half the battle."

"Here," he said, coming to his feet. "I'll show you a good one."

"No thanks." She turned away, shaking her head, but he moved too quickly for her.

"If someone grabs you, like this," he said, coming up behind her and sliding his arms in, locking them just beneath her breasts, pulling her close in against him. "What would you do?"

She gasped. His face was next to hers, his breath tantalizing her cheek, his rough day's growth of beard rasping against her skin. It had all happened so fast, she had to wait a beat or two to make sure she understood just exactly what was going on here.

"You snap back your right elbow and at the same time, you make a turn to the left," he was advising, his voice silky, so very near her ear.

She could hardly breathe. He was holding her to his

long, strong body and she thought she could feel every
one of his muscles against her back. Her natural in-
clination was to do as he said and turn toward the left,
but one second of clear thinking and she realized what
that meant. She might be in his arms now, but if she
followed his instructions she would be in his embrace
and in perfect position to be kissed.

A lovely thought—if only she could believe he
wasn't doing this on purpose just to mock her. Which,
of course, he was! She steeled herself. She wasn't going to follow through and fall into his trap. Instead,
she made another move her personal defense trainer
had taught her and quickly raised her foot, coming
down hard on top of his.

He yelled. She pulled out of his grip, whirling to
glare at him hotly. Half-laughing, he was hobbling in
pain.

"My God, woman, you're lethal. I was just trying
to show you…"

She raised her hands as though to defend herself.
"Stay back!" she ordered him.

And at the same time, the cook came bustling in
through the outer doorway, her hair damp, her look
very cross. She took in the scene at a glance, nodded
at Tianna, and glared daggers at the man standing beside her.

"Young mister, you know the rules," she said
sternly, shaking a finger at him. "There's to be no
trifling with the help." She all but stamped her foot
and pointed to show him the way out of her kitchen.

"Trifling?" He glanced at Tianna and shook his head, laughing softly. "Don't worry. This lady is definitely a no-trifling zone."

His gaze met hers and held for a moment, then he turned his full charm on the cook.

"That you, of all people, should accuse me of trifling." He had the confident smile of a man who had used charisma as his currency out of many a sticky situation in his life and was pretty sure it would work for him again, any time he chose to use it. "I was doing no such thing. I was merely keeping a visitor company while waiting for you to return and do your duty by her."

The cook was still pointing. "If you want to practice your profligate ways, you'll do so somewhere else," she insisted. "I've got work to do here."

The handsome charmer reacted with weary resignation.

"Aye aye, Cook." He gave her a somewhat disjointed salute, then leaned toward her teasingly. "My mentor, my conscience, my guide. As ever, words of wisdom fall from your lips like petals from the rose...."

The cook colored and had a hard time not showing pleasure at his affectionate mockery. "Get on with you." She swatted at him with a dish towel, but she was beaming in a way that gave full evidence to how much she cared for him. "And keep your crazy poetry to yourself."

"Hey, watch that talk," he said as he prepared to

depart. "You know I have to maintain my reputation as a soldier. Don't start spreading that poetry rumor."

He stopped to drop a quick kiss on the cook's cheek, then dodged another swipe with the dish towel as he made his way toward the exit. Tianna noted with a twinge of guilty satisfaction that he was limping slightly. He paused in the doorway, looking back.

"Goodbye, lovely lady," he said to Tianna just before disappearing out the door. "I hope we meet again." A fleeting smile, and then he was gone.

Tianna thought she'd probably seen the last of him and was disappointed in herself for caring. She had to admit, it would be tempting to let herself get a healthy crush on a man like that, to start thinking about the scent of roses and kisses in the moonlight. The only love affair she'd let herself attempt had ended badly and had seemed hardly worth the effort in the end. She had the feeling things might have been different with a man like this.

"He's got a heart of gold, that one," the cook confided once he was out of the room. "But he does tease so."

Tianna smiled, her pulse still reacting to the man's presence in the room. "Is he your son?"

The cook looked shocked. "My son? Heaven's no. My dear, don't you know who that is? Why, it's Prince Garth, that's who."

Chapter Two

Tianna felt the room fade and pulse, and she barely avoided a gasp. "Prince Garth!" She put her hand over her heart. "But…but the little maid told me the prince had gone to Texas."

"Oh, aye. She thought you meant Crown Prince Marco, no doubt about it. He was here last week." She began to bustle about the kitchen. "No one thinks of Garth as 'the prince.' He's always been the younger brother, you know. The rascal. The charming one." She grinned affectionately.

Tianna sat, still dumbfounded, and growing more and more astonished as she thought over this latest wrinkle. So the man they expected her to marry really was a playboy and a carouser. Delightfully irresistible—and the last man in the world a woman would want to be married to. Hah! Just wait until she explained all this to her father. It looked like she would be able to put together a nice tight case for annulling this betrothal. And wasn't that what she'd come for?

Actually, it was getting hard to remember what she'd come for. Too much was getting in the way.

The cook had turned back and was frowning down at her. "Well, now about your business. Come about the pastry chef job, have you? We weren't expecting you quite this soon, but that's all right. We'll make do."

Tianna turned to tell her the truth, but she was rattling on.

"Now, let's see a bit of your talent. I've got some dough mixed for pies. Why don't you roll it out and we'll see what you can do with it. Try something creative."

"I'm really not here for the pastry chef job."

"No?"

"No. I'm…"

It was going to be hard to explain what she was here for at this point—and why she hadn't talked to Garth when she had a chance. Her day was careening wildly out of control. It was probably time she made herself known to everyone and tried to get some order back into things. "Actually, you see, I'm Princess Katianna of…"

Unfortunately, her words were drowned out by the sudden wail of the infant. The cook whirled and stared at the basket on the table.

"A baby!" Cook's gaze fell on the basket. "Ah yes, Milla said you'd brought your baby. We really don't have facilities for babies here. You should have asked first, you know."

Tianna considered tearing her hair out, but thought better of it. "She's not my baby," she said evenly. "I found her in the yard."

Cook rolled her eyes. "What nonsense," she said, and bent over the little thing, cooing to it.

Tianna bit her lip and silently counted to ten, then drew herself up and gazed coolly at the woman. "I assure you, I'm telling the truth."

Cook glanced up and seemed to recognize her growing irritation. "Well, that's as may be. But then where did this baby come from?"

Good question. If only someone would answer it! Stifling the urge to scream, Tianna gave her a quick explanation of how the estate had been left unguarded and open to the world when she'd arrived. The cook finally seemed to accept that, though reluctantly.

"Oh yes, we're so shorthanded right now, things are falling to wrack and ruin," she said, shaking her head. "You know, they usually leave their babies at the guard gate. We never even see them up here. And you say you found her right out in the garden?"

Tianna frowned. "Are you telling me strange babies show up here all the time?" she asked.

Cook shrugged. "Well, not all the time. But it's been known to happen. Single girls hoping we'll take the tykes in and raise them as royals. Surely you know about the legend of Baby Rose. It's an old Nabotavian story.''

She didn't, but she wasn't in the mood for a story right now. ''You think this one was left by a desperate young girl?'' she asked, looking down at the dewy little face and wishing she didn't feel such a strong emotional pull every time she did so. The baby was starting to fuss again and she pulled it up into her arms without thinking twice, patting her little back and whispering sweet nothings against her silky head.

''No doubt about it.'' The cook turned and spoke to the kitchen maid. ''Milla, call the orphanage. Tell them we'll be sending another baby over.''

Tianna looked up, frowning. She hated to think of letting this little angel go. ''Don't you think we should call the police? And perhaps, Children's Services?''

''Children's Services? Oh my, no. We'll call the Nabotavian Orphanage, that's what we'll do. They'll take her. We Nabotavians like to take care of our own.'' She frowned at Tianna. ''Aren't you a daughter of the Rose nation, my dear?''

''Yes, of course I am.''

''Been in this country a little too long, though, haven't you? Started to think like an American. Just like my young prince. It's a good thing we'll all be going back soon.'' She shook her head. ''We've almost lost our heritage, I do declare.''

''So you're preparing for the return?''

''We're at sixes and sevens, my dear. All this moving back to Nabotavia has the entire staff in an uproar.'' She looked overwhelmed by it all. ''The house-keeper left a week ago to manage the preparations at Red Rose Palace and she took some of our best workers with her. She left Mr. Harva, the butler, in charge, and he immediately ran off with the pastry chef. Now I'm left to try to keep things from falling apart here, and heaven knows I have my hands full.''

The little maid returned at that moment, walking into the kitchen with a bouncy step. ''The orphanage can't take her. They've got chicken pox. They can't take anyone new for at least four days.''

''Oh my heavens! What's next?'' The cook turned to Tianna, shaking her head.

Tianna looked from the cook to the baby and back again. Hesitating, she recognized that she was at a crossroads. She could hand the baby back and identify herself, and everything would change. She would be the princess and escorted to the other side of the house where she would be given a beautiful bedroom for the night and probably not see this baby again.

Or she could let them think she was a mere job seeker and stick around for a while. She looked down into the baby's face. The lower lip was trembling and the huge blue eyes were clouded. A wave of protective affection seized her. The child felt so soft and snuggly and she smelled like something fresh and new—which was exactly what she was. But she was also so helpless. Tianna hadn't been quite this young, but she had known what it was to be helpless and lost. She didn't wish that on anyone, especially not this innocent.

Someone had to make sure nothing bad happened to her. And since she'd had plenty of experience helping with her sister's baby, she supposed she was the one to do it.

"I…well, I suppose I could help…."

"And what is your name, child?"

Her chin lifted. "Tianna Rose." It was the name she went by in daily life, and would do for the moment. No one would connect it to the Katianna Roseanova-Krimorova who was betrothed to the prince.

"Ah, a Rose, are you?" The cook nodded knowingly. "Related to the royal family by any chance?"

Tianna met her gaze levelly but she wasn't prepared to outright lie. "Perhaps."

"Ah, yes. Everyone likes to claim a little relationship here and there." The cook smiled sympathetically. "I'm sure you have the usual references. Well, we can put you to work, I think. Somebody is going to have to take care of this baby, and I don't dare let Milla do it. She'd probably leave it out in the yard again." She smiled hopefully. "What do you know about the nanny business, Tianna Rose?"

For Prince Garth, driving his Porsche was a major part of the joy of life. Sleek and silver, his car purred like a giant cat and was so responsive to his handling, it reminded him of a sensual woman. Maybe that was why, as he drove up the winding driveway, returning from an afternoon of boring meetings in town with lawyers and business managers, his thoughts went to the lovely woman he'd met that morning in the gazebo.

He could still feel the way her curves had fit against his body and the memory stirred his reactions in a way that made him laugh at himself. She was certainly a tempting bit of luscious femininity—which should put him on guard, as he'd recently sworn off women altogether.

Women! They never played fair. Even those who agreed to ground rules from the beginning—vowing to keep things light and playful, swearing there would be no hearts involved, ended up wanting commitments and long-range promises in the end. And if you rebuffed their come-on advances, they usually found a way to make you pay.

He was still reeling from his last scandal involving a woman he hadn't even kissed. She'd told the tabloids a wild tale of sex in public places and orgies on yachts and all because he'd stopped taking her phone calls. Sometimes you couldn't win for losing.

On the other hand, he hated to think of how many women he'd hurt over the years. But their hearts seemed to break so easily. He'd finally come to the conclusion that it was better just to stay completely out of the game. After all, he was betrothed. He didn't need to search for a mate, so why not give up women for the time being?

Still, the lovely yet dangerous visitor intrigued him. She'd said she was a photographer, yet all evidence suggested she was here to apply for the pastry chef position. Hopefully, she was going to be preparing tempting confections for him from now on. That thought made him smile again. Leaving his car out front for Homer, the chauffeur, to deal with, he went straight into the kitchen and greeted Cook with a peck on the cheek.

"There you are," she said in a harried fashion. "Will you be having your dinner here tonight, then?"

"Yes, I think I will." He glanced around the kitchen but didn't catch sight of the woman he was searching for.

"Good." Cook gave him a baleful look. "You've been out gallivanting too much lately. It'll do you good to stay at home for a change. Any guests?"

"No." He peered around the kitchen, noting Milla shelling peas and a thin stranger cleaning off a counter. "What happened to the new pastry chef?"

Cook nodded in the direction of the slender woman. "There she is. She's hard at work."

Garth did a double take and frowned. "No, I mean the other one." He turned to the older woman in alarm. "You didn't hire her?"

"Oh, that one." She waved a hand in the air. "Tianna, you mean. Yes, she's still here. She agreed to be nanny to that baby that was found in the yard, at least until the orphanage can take her—or someone shows up to claim her. She's probably up in the nursery right now…"

But Garth was already on his way, whistling as he went. Tianna. So that was her name. A lovely and typically Nabotavian name, a lovely and typically Nabotavian girl. Against all his better judgements, he was looking forward to seeing her again. Although he had a rather inflated reputation as a playboy, he had never actually dallied with the help. It wasn't his style. But then, the help had never been quite so beautiful before. There was always the exception that proved the rule.

He was feeling rather debonair as he knocked a quick rhythm on the nursery room door.

"Come in," her voice called.

He straightened his tie and turned the knob, a provocative smile at the ready. But when he opened the door, instead of the welcoming look of surprise he expected, he found himself gazing into a face that, though still beautiful, was set in a look that said "trouble."

"There you are!" she exclaimed.

He stopped in his tracks, but at least she didn't have her dukes up this time. "What did I do?" he asked, completely at sea.

She gave him a look that said, "If you don't know..." and rose from the rocking chair with the baby in her arms.

"I've been waiting for you to come home," she said distractedly. "I've got to talk to you."

He raised an eyebrow, surprised at her tone but happy to see she was every bit as lovely as he remembered. Her soft burnished hair set off a face that was finely boned, the lips full, the green eyes luminous and framed in thick dark lashes. He liked the look of her and he was already speculating what her touch would be like.

"I had some meetings to attend to. And very tedious they were, too. Why? Did I miss something?"

Did he miss something!

Turning, she carefully laid the sleeping baby down in its antique crib, giving herself a moment to compose her emotions. Trailing a finger across the downy head, she felt a surge of affection for this helpless creature that was beginning to seem automatic. She looked so beautiful tucked under her lacy covers. It was official now. Tianna was her defender and protector. She would do whatever she had to do to make sure this child was safe and well taken care of.

Luckily, the nursery was fully stocked with baby supplies, as it had only been a short time since Prince Marco's two children had passed through on their way to their larger bedrooms. Milla had been sent into town to get formula and baby food, but disposable diapers and baby blankets filled the cupboards—everything a well-connected baby would need. And this sweet baby might just be a little more well-connected than everyone had first believed.

Turning, she looked at Prince Garth. She'd been sitting here for the past few hours working herself up into a lather over this situation and it wasn't going to help if she started ranting at him. At any rate, now that they were face-to-face, she knew he wasn't the monster she'd been painting in her mind. Surely he would do the right thing.

"Have you done anything yet to find the mother of this baby?" she asked carefully.

He seemed puzzled by her question but he answered readily enough. "Don't worry about that. The authorities will handle it. The orphanage finds the mothers very quickly. The mothers and babies are usually reunited within days." He shook his head. "They do this because of the Rose Baby Legend, you know."

She paused, biting her lip. This legend had been mentioned twice. It had to be peculiar to East Nabotavia, because she didn't remember ever hearing of it before. She supposed she ought to get the full background before she made her case.

"Why don't you sit down?" she suggested, gesturing toward a chair set facing the rocker. "I'd like to hear about this Rose Baby Legend."

He looked at her and almost laughed. She was talking to him as though…hell, as though she were a princess. Actually, he was used to people treating him with casual equality. After all, he'd spent quite a few years in the U.S. Army after graduating from West Point, the last few as a lieutenant colonel. But this was different. He was in his own home castle and Tianna was an employee. By now she surely knew he was a prince. It was very strange that she didn't seem to feel a need to treat him like—well, at least like the boss. A neutral observer might have come to the opposite conclusion and figured *he* must work for *her*.

"You're Nabotavian, aren't you?" he asked as he

sank easily into the chair. "Surely you've heard the story."

"I may have heard it once, but if I did, it didn't stick with me." She sat down in the rocker and leaned forward. "Why don't you fill me in?"

"The Rose Baby Legend. Okay." He frowned, calling up the old story from the past. "It started about a hundred years ago in Nabotavia. It was a time of great instability in the kingdom—as usual. The queen—my great-grandmother—had given birth to three boys and then found she was unable to have any more children. She desperately wanted a girl. In fact, supposedly she'd fallen into deep depression because, as she said, the boys would all be taken from her by war and she deeply longed for a daughter who would stay beside her always. Everyone in the country knew about her sorrow. Then one day, while walking in the rose garden, she found a baby girl, wrapped in a rose-colored blanket. She adopted her, raised her as her own, even to the point of calling her a princess. She was my great aunt, Princess Elna. True to the queen's desires, she never married, staying with her adoptive mother to the end."

"Wow."

"Yes. You don't see that kind of gratitude much these days, do you?" He gave her a crooked grin. "I don't really remember her, but I've always heard a lot about her. She affected the lives of all she came in contact with. She was the first one to start a nursing charity for the poor. She founded the original Nabotavian orphanage. The whole country loved her. She was considered a sort of royal saint.''

"Princess Elna.'' Tianna nodded. She remembered now. She'd read a biography of the woman when she was about twelve or thirteen. "Yes, of course. I've heard of her. She was a wonderful woman.''

"Yes. Anyway, she became quite a legend, and eventually a myth grew up around her experience. It was thought that the royal family might take in other babies. The rose garden was open to the public in those days and women began leaving their babies there, with notes, begging for the royal family to adopt the baby. For some reason, a few years ago, the story was revived and they started trying to do that here, too. They usually don't get any farther than the guard gate, though.''

"I see.'' She nodded thoughtfully, then glanced at the crib where the little girl slept.

Garth followed her gaze. "Now where was it you found her?'' he asked, watching for her reaction.

Tianna looked at him. "Just outside, along the driveway.''

"Not in the rose garden?''

"No, it was among the primroses.''

She blinked and their eyes met. His eyebrow cocked.

"Too bad,'' he said softly. "I'm afraid we're not in the adopting mood here at the castle.''

Tianna's gaze was still holding his. "What if it's

not just some stranger who left her?'' she asked softly. ''What if it's someone you know?''

He frowned, sitting back in his chair. The wary look returned to his handsome face. ''What are you driving at?''

She rose, stepping to the chest of drawers and returning with a small note card. Even from where he was sitting, he could smell the rose scent it had been dabbed with.

''Here,'' she said. ''You'd better read this. It fell out of the baby's clothing.''

He looked at it for a moment, a feeling of unease growing in his chest. This had all the earmarks of something that was going to be extremely unpleasant. Reluctantly, he reached for the card.

''My dearest Garth,'' the note began. He groaned softly, then went on reading.

''Why have you done this to me? You never come by and you don't write anymore. I'm at my wits' end. I don't know what to do. I can't handle this by myself. It's just too hard. I feel I've lost your love and your support. But this baby is as much yours as she is mine. I'm leaving her for you to raise. I just can't do it on my own. But I still love you and always will. Your Sunshine Girl.''

''Nice try, Sunshine Girl,'' he said sardonically, flipping the letter down on the small table between them. He took a deep breath, then looked up into Tianna's intense green gaze. ''I assume you read this.''

"I…" She flushed, realizing she had intruded herself where she hadn't been invited. "I'm sorry, but I thought…"

"Of course you read it," he said, sweeping away her apologies. "That hardly matters." He fixed her with a serious look. "What does matter is that you realize it's a hoax."

"A hoax?"

"Of course." He looked at the paper as though he could start a flame if he stared hard enough. "I have no idea who this person is. And I'm not the father of her baby."

Tianna stared at him. So this was the angle he was going to take. For some reason, she'd thought he might respond with remorse at least, and hopefully promises of support. But as she looked into his clear blue eyes, she could see that he had no intention of doing any such thing.

For the first time since she'd read the note, her confidence wavered. Maybe he was right. Maybe the baby wasn't his. On one level, she would like to believe it. But how could that be? The note came across as so sincere. And women usually knew who the fathers of their babies were. It was hard for her to believe that any woman would set her baby out to be found like that without being darn sure….

"I assumed at least you would know who she is," she said, pinning him with a penetrating look.

"No. I do not know who this is."

She leaned forward, frowning. The baby seemed to

be about four months old to her. "Well, if you think back…. Where were you a little over a year ago? That's when it would have happened."

"I was in Nabotavia," he said coolly. "Fighting with the underground."

"Oh." She sat back. That certainly put a different light on the subject. Still… "But maybe she was in Nabotavia, too."

A muscle twitched at his temple and his mouth seemed to harden. "And maybe she's just a local girl who heard about the Rose Baby Legend and decided to take her chances."

She held his gaze with her own intense stare. "Maybe."

They stayed that way for a long moment as the air crackled between them. Suddenly Tianna was short of breath and afraid she knew exactly why. She licked her lips, trying to mask her breathlessness, and saw his gaze darken as he followed the path of her tongue. That only made things worse. She had to focus hard to remember what they were here talking about.

"At any rate, there's no need for you to worry about it," he said at last, shrugging carelessly. "I'm sure the mother will be found eventually."

She drew in a sharp breath, back on subject and exasperated with him. "That's all you have to say about this?"

He looked very continental and above it all. "What would you like me to say?"

She shrugged, growing more and more annoyed

with him. "Oh, I don't know. Maybe that you're sorry the poor little thing has been abandoned. That you'll make some effort to find out where she belongs." She threw out her arms. "How about giving some indication that just possibly you might give a damn?"

But what if I don't?

He didn't say it, but he was tempted to, more because he knew it would drive her crazy than anything else. Of course he cared on a basic human level. But that was pretty abstract. In the grand scheme of things, he had to admit that the women who left their babies hoping the royals would raise them didn't interest him much. It had been happening for as long as he could remember. The only thing that made this instance different was that this new mother had composed a bogus note to add to the mix—and that Tianna was involved.

He had to admit, she interested him more than any woman had in a long time. Women usually swooned around him, flirted, gushed, gave every indication that they would love to be taken home and ravished. But Tianna was different. She reacted enough to let him know she wasn't immune to the attraction that had sprung up between them from the first. But she was working very hard to resist it. And that, of course, was a challenge he might not be able to ignore.

Still, he knew she wasn't going to be happy until he took some steps toward solving the problem of the baby—an annoyance he could easily take care of.

"If it will make you feel better, I'll put a real expert on the case right away." He pulled out his cell phone and quickly punched in a number. "Janus? I have an assignment for you. Please meet me in the study in…oh, say five minutes."

"My valet," he told her as he folded his phone and put it away in his pocket. "He's the most trustworthy man I know. He'll handle it."

She sat very still and drew in a slow, deep breath. Where should she go from here? It would have been nice to see more enthusiasm from him, more interest in getting to the bottom of this mystery. It disappointed her to have him brush it off, as if it hardly mattered, as if, like any rich and powerful person, he didn't have to deal with the problems of the little people. This was exactly what she hated about the monarchy—and one of the main reasons she was determined to slough it off like a poorly fitting skin.

He rose from his chair and she rose to face him. "Would you like to hold the baby before you go?" she asked hopefully.

His eyes shone with a quizzical sheen. "No thanks," he said dismissively. He hesitated, then added, "Dinner is at six in the game room."

"Oh, I can't leave the baby."

He looked pained. "Of course you can. I'll send up Bridget, the downstairs maid, to sit with the baby. She often watches Marcos's children."

"No, I really don't think…"

"Tianna."

Her head jerked up at the tone of his voice. He hadn't come right out and said, "Listen, wench, I think you're forgetting who's in charge here,'' but he might as well have. The implication was clear as a bell.

"I require your presence at dinner," he said, his voice low but filled with steel. "Six o'clock in the game room."

She swallowed and stared at him, suddenly tongue-tied. His face softened into a lazy, knowing smile that managed to leave her feeling caressed, though he hadn't touched her.

"We need some time to get to know each other better," he added, his voice hinting at promises of something unexpressed but easy enough to understand.

Catching her breath, she watched while he left the room, then she stared at the door after he'd closed it behind him.

"There's your problem," she whispered to herself, shaking her head in a sort of wonder. "You're letting the man hypnotize you. Cut it out!" Groaning, she turned back to check on the child.

Not many men had ever managed to penetrate her sometimes cool exterior armor. And she was thankful for that. She had the example of her younger sister, Jannika, to show her how bad things could get. Janni had not only found a way to sneak out on dates, she'd married someone her family disapproved of, had a baby and been abandoned by her young shiftless husband and was now living at home again—a fate so filled with regret and shame that Tianna would have died rather than copy it.

She'd grown up in a bookish sort of household, where trips to the library were more important than trips to the mall. On vacations, her family made reservations at museums rather than at the trendiest hot spots. She'd gone to girls' schools, and even her college had been mostly female. The few times people of the male gender had appeared on her horizon, there had always been a sense of distance, because after all, she was betrothed.

That arrangement had seemed to be the magic spell that kept her from harm for a long, long time. But once she'd begun to take her photography classes, and become quite good at it, she'd realized that the very thing that had served as her shield now acted as her jailer. As long as she was promised to the Nabotavian prince, she was tied to the monarchy, tied to certain duties and responsibilities—and would never be allowed to take off for New York to pursue her photography dream.

So she'd taken a step off the reservation. The recipe was an old one. Take one handsome and worldly instructor and one innocent but curious student, give them time alone together, and poof! One quick pulse-pounding love affair to go.

Luckily she'd pulled back from the brink in time to save herself from complete insanity—as well as from her sister's fate. But she felt she knew a lot more about men and sensual chemistry now. And she knew it could ruin your life if you let it. But she wasn't interested in affairs of the heart any more than she was interested in playing the princess part. She was a photographer.

Despite what her father might think, evidence suggested she really did have a lot of talent. She'd submitted entries to contests, won a few, and finally received a job offer in Chicago that she was determined to take. It wasn't quite New York, but it was on the way. Opening that envelope with the offer inside had been the most exciting thing she'd ever done.

Her father, of course, had scorned it. "It's of no use to you. You'll be marrying Prince Garth soon," he'd said.

She found it a little odd that he'd brought it up, actually. He hadn't said much about it over the years. As a family, they hadn't kept up ties with the Nabotavian community to any large extent. So she'd begun to think maybe it wasn't all that important any longer. And she was perfectly happy to ignore it—until it loomed as a barrier to something she really wanted to do. She had to remember that she'd come to find a way to break her engagement, and she couldn't let a momentary attraction to the very man from whom she wanted to break free deter her from her goal.

"Oh well," she told herself with forced cheer. "By the time I make him take responsibility for this baby, he might be so sick of me, he'll be glad to see me go!"

She could only hope.

Chapter Three

Tianna entered the game room at exactly six. She came in slowly, warily, scanning the room for danger. She was so busy being careful, she didn't see Prince Garth standing just behind her and she jumped when he spoke.

"Good evening."

"Oh!" She turned quickly and tried to pretend she hadn't been startled. "Good evening," she said, nervously smoothing down the lacy collar at her neck. The dress she wore was long and clinging, buttoned high at the neck and decorated with white lace. It was like nothing she ever wore in her real life, but she hadn't brought much in her overnight case, and she'd been told she could wear anything she found in the nanny's closet. Luckily, at least one of the previous nannies had been very close to her size, if not to her taste in clothes.

The prince was dressed casually, but with understated elegance, the crease in his slacks so sharp it could have cut wood, the fabric of his white shirt so soft, it clung to the hard lines of his muscular torso. The virility of the man made her heart jump and she couldn't avoid backing up a step as he came toward her, just because his appeal was so darn scary.

"Won't you sit down?" he said smoothly, gesturing toward two chairs set up at the other end of the room. "I thought you might like to have a drink before dinner."

"Where are the others?" she asked, looking about the room suspiciously.

"There are no others," he told her, giving her a significant half smile, "We're it."

She hesitated, looking at him sideways, perfectly willing to let him understand that she didn't trust him. "I don't know about this," she said archly.

"Sure you do," he replied, taking her hand and bringing it to his lips. "I've invited you down here to seduce you," he said, his eyes ravishing her in a mocking way. "It's perfectly obvious. I do this with all the nannies. Sort of an initiation ceremony, if you like."

She gave him a long-suffering look. He was teasing her again and she wasn't going to fall for it. Still, she did reclaim her hand and turned to look at the room again. Paneled in dark wood and lined with tall bookcases, it sported card and gaming tables, along with a large green felt billiard table and a huge fireplace at one end. The two wing chairs with a small coffee table between them faced the fireplace.

"About that drink," he began.

"I thought you'd given up alcohol," she said, eyebrows raised.

"I have." He gestured toward the coffee table set between the chairs where she could see a ceramic pot and two delicate cups waiting. "I'm having green tea. Good for the digestion. You can join me, or I'll have Janus bring you something else."

She looked at him, not totally convinced of his reformation. He was still laughing at her. She didn't know if that irked her or made her want to laugh, too.

"Green tea would be lovely," she said.

He offered her a seat with a flourish and she gracefully lowered herself into it, then leaned forward and began to serve the tea. He stared at her for a moment, startled. The nanny didn't usually take it upon herself to go ahead and serve the tea without being asked to do so. She was acting as though *she* were the hostess, completely comfortable in the role—as though this was what she normally did. He frowned. Nothing about this woman fell into patterns for him. She was unusual, to say the least. Unusual, and somewhat annoying.

As he sank into the opposite chair, he wondered why she seemed to be able to get under his skin in a way no other woman ever had. He knew very well that he was not the father of that baby she was now so fiercely guarding, and yet he'd spent the entire afternoon racking his brain, trying to remember every contact he'd had, every woman he'd dated, every night he might have had too much to drink to remember what he was doing.

But the last didn't happen very often these days. And even when it had in the past, he never really lost control. Which was the main reason he was pretty confident nothing could happen, no big surprise could fall out of the sky, no young woman who called herself his Sunshine Girl could appear and provide proof that he was the guilty party. Because there was no such girl.

And still, Tianna's reproachful looks made him think twice every time. At any rate, she had played havoc with his emotional equilibrium since the first moment he'd woken to find her standing beside where he slept in the gazebo, like a vision, a manifestation of his dreams. He grimaced. This wasn't like him. It had to stop.

But never mind. He was used to dealing with women. Surely he could handle even this.

He accepted the cup of tea she offered, then raised it in a mock salute. "To love and beauty," he toasted.

Her eyes flashed and she raised her own cup. "To integrity," she countered, making him sputter on his first sip.

"Tianna," he began warningly. "You're much too beautiful to waste your time being a nag."

A nag! Setting down her cup, she sat back and crossed her arms, gazing at him levelly. "I think we had better get something straight. You seem to have quite a reputation as a playboy. But I'm not a plaything. And I'm not here to play around.''

She thought she sounded wonderfully confident and that was good. If only she felt as sure as she sounded. But whenever she looked at him, she sensed she was walking on quicksand. Humor simmered in his gaze, but something else was lurking there as well. She wasn't sure what it was, but she knew it was making her very nervous.

''Never say never, Tianna,'' he advised in his most world-weary tone. ''In the long run, everything's negotiable.''

''No.'' Slowly, she shook her head, her eyes clear and bright. ''You're wrong. Some things are just too important for that.''

He shrugged. She would learn with time and experience.

They chatted about inconsequential things for a few minutes and then Janus came in carrying the soup course. She smiled a greeting his way. A tall, handsome man in his late forties, Janus had come by the nursery that afternoon once Garth had filled him in on the particulars. He was a gentle-looking man with something of a twinkle in his eyes. He had gone right to the baby when she'd let him in, lifted her up and spoke soothingly to her.

''I can see you've had babies of your own,'' she'd said, smiling. Her own skills came from helping her sister. She had never realized how much she would come to rely on what she'd learned there.

"Oh no, I've never married," he said. "But I have plenty of nieces and nephews. I know my way around a nursery."

She was reassured to know that he shared her concern for the little one. She could see that he loved children and she'd felt a lot better about putting the investigation in his hands.

"Dinner is served," he said now, bowing graciously.

Prince Garth offered Tianna his arm and they went to the table which had been set up in the middle of the room. The service was informal but still stunning, the sterling silver heavy, the bone china fragile as eggshells, the crystal glittering in the lamplight. Janus ladled out shrimp bisque and went back to the kitchen to prepare the second course.

"I'm impressed with your valet," she said as he left the room.

Garth nodded. "Janus is a multifaceted man. Not only does he keep me from falling off the edge of the earth on occasion, he's also quite the amateur artist. Oils, mostly. He spends most of his free time down at the artists' colony in Sedona." He smiled at her. "If you play your cards right, he'll do your portrait."

"That would be lovely." She thought of the official portrait that hung in her family's library. She was dressed as Diana, goddess of the hunt, for some strange reason. The artist who had done the work liked to see life in terms of Olympian gods. She'd loved it when she was eighteen. Now, it was just plain embarrassing.

And then Garth said something, rather softly, that stopped her in her tracks.

"Janus is the one who rescued me during the revolt and brought me to America," he said, adding simply, "I owe my life to him."

They were both silent for a moment. Tianna was remembering that his parents had been murdered in the revolution. He must have been a young boy when that happened. Suddenly, she felt a wave of sympathy for him. The history of her country was full of tragedies and his was just another one. But something in his eyes told her the tragedy lived in him still.

"Tell me a little about yourself," he said as though to fill the quiet space. "Where have you been living?"

"I was raised in the Seattle area," she said after a brief hesitation. Giving the location might set off a chain of recognition in him. After all, not many Nabotavians lived in the Pacific Northwest.

In fact, she sometimes thought her parents had taken the entire sojourn in America as a welcome respite from the responsibilities and duties of leading a regional state. She and her sister and brother had been brought up in a very nice well-to-do neighborhood in suburban Seattle. But their house had been no grander than anyone else's on the block. No one except very close friends had even known they had royal connections. She'd had a pretty normal childhood. There had been an estate manager and some minimal security, just in case, but for the most part, they hadn't had any more servants than any of their wealthy neighbors.

So admitting to living in the north might sound odd to him, might even make him wonder. But she wasn't going to lie. So if it did, it did.

But he gave no sign of surprise. "So you went to school there?"

"Yes. To a small college just outside the city."

He nodded, buttering a roll. "You have something of the Seattle look."

"Tweedy and damp?" she asked, laughing.

"Not at all. It's that vigorous youth thing, well-educated and interested in the world around you."

She colored slightly. It seemed to be a sincere comment and she appreciated it. "I'd return the compliment and say you have an Arizona look, but I'm not really sure what that would be."

"Sunburnt and wind-whipped," he said, dismissing it. "You said you were a photographer, didn't you? Tell me about that. What got you started?"

She hesitated, but once she got going, there seemed to be a lot she had to say on the subject. He sat back, nodding at Janus as he took the soup plates and set out the salmon, listening to her with only part of his attention, while the rest was engaged in a study of this puzzling female.

He was becoming more and more entranced by her careless, yet luminous beauty. He liked the way her eyes lit up while she was talking about the profession she was learning to love, the way she used her hands to emphasize a point. He liked the way the white collar gave her a virginal look that was undercut by the generous proportions she displayed beneath the dark dress that hugged her curves. And the way the silver clasp that was holding back her hair was falling out, letting strands slide free to curl around her face.

For just a moment he wondered what it would be like if he weren't royal. Would he be dating women like this? There was something very appealing about that thought.

Soon he would be heading back to Nabotavia to take his place among the leadership of his native country. He'd been there during the fight to throw off the rebels the year before, but he'd been incognito, fighting with the underground, helping the effort that was ultimately sweet in its complete success. He'd thought that defeating the thugs who'd killed his parents and stolen his birthright would change everything. But it really hadn't. The hole in his heart was still there. Maybe it just wasn't meant to heal.

"I think we should talk about the baby for a moment," she said suddenly.

He frowned, jolted back from his reverie. "If we must," he murmured.

She nodded resolutely. "Putting Janus in charge of the investigation was a great move."

"So you're happy now?"

She gave him a look very close to outrage. "Certainly not."

He sighed. "And why is that?"

She leaned toward him. "Janus is wonderful. But can't you see that you should be doing the searching yourself? In some way or other, you seem to be responsible for this baby's existence."

His mouth tightened and his fingers began playing with the silverware. "So you want me to do what exactly?"

Taking a deep breath, she said, "I think you should be a little more hands-on in looking for the mother. After all, you probably know her."

"I don't know her."

Her voice rose with the intensity of her passion for this subject. "How do you know that when we don't know who she is?"

His eyes flashed. "You know what? You're the most insubordinate employee this castle has ever had."

"Good. It's about time someone told you the truth, isn't it?"

They glared at one another for a moment, and then Prince Garth's anger faded. "Tianna," he said quietly, "calm down. There's no need to get excited about this. We're not adversaries. I'm not trying to put one over on you in any way." He smiled at her. "I'm not even really trying to seduce you."

"Hah!" she said, her own smile wobbling. "You had me believing you there until that last bit."

He laughed, but she laughed along with him. And

she realized he was right. Why was she so on the defensive with him? He was just a man, after all.

Taking a deep breath, she tried to center her emotions. She'd come here to make an ally out of him, not an enemy. She still hoped that he would join her in nullifying this silly betrothal. For now, she'd gotten shanghaied into taking care of the baby, but that was okay. The baby came first. Once she was certain the little sweetheart's future was assured, there would be time to deal with her own life. She would get much further if she took it all on an even keel. After all, he was just a man.

Then she took another look at him and fell back into the reality zone. Who was she kidding? Of course she had to be on guard with him. He was so darn gorgeous, so charming, so desirable. She was like a girl who'd been denied ice cream staring at a large bowl of French vanilla. With hot fudge dripping over it. Steeling herself to resist temptation, she turned back to him.

"You're right," she said. "Truce?"

He held out his hand and she hesitantly put her hand in his. "Truce," he said in a low husky voice that made her want to whimper.

Luckily, Janus arrived with dessert, two small cups of crème brûlée, and the tone lightened quickly. By the time they had finished the delicious custard, Garth had launched into an explanation of the preparations for the return to Nabotavia. To her surprise, he seemed quite enthusiastic about it.

"But don't you think the monarchy has had its day?" she said to him at last. "They've become nothing but fodder for the tabloids."

"That may be the way it is in some countries, but Nabotavia is going to be different." He said it with such authority, she had to think he really believed it. "My brother Marco and I have been preparing for this all our lives. We're going to be running that country and we're going to run it right."

She shook her head. "Well, I'm glad *you're* so optimistic about going back and ruling. But as for me…"

"You?"

She bit her tongue. She'd forgotten he didn't know she was just as royal as he was.

He leaned forward, looking at her. "Are you planning to join the return?"

She quickly shook her head. "Not me. I told you, I'm a photographer. I have a job lined up in Chicago."

"Really?" He gazed at her speculatively. "Then why were you here applying for a job as a pastry chef?"

She opened her mouth and then closed it again. Oops. The way things had turned out, it would be best to pretend she had been after the pastry chef job after all. "Uh… I just needed a job to tide me over for a bit, before my position in Chicago starts," she improvised quickly, her heart sinking as she spoke. "So taking care of the baby for a few days will be perfect," she added lamely.

He stared at her, hard. He distinctly remembered her saying she hadn't come for the pastry chef job, but she had never really explained what she *had* come for.

"Who are you, Tianna?" he asked softly, searching her eyes. "Where did you come from?"

"I told you. Seattle."

"What is your last name?" the prince asked, still looking at her curiously.

"Rose," she said, stealing herself again.

"Rose!" He frowned at her in alarm. "Is that short for Roseanova?"

"Roseanova is not my last name." And that wasn't a fib. It was the next to her last name, but not the last one.

"Good. I was suddenly afraid you might have been one of my crazy cousins." He sighed. "A flock of them is descending upon us tomorrow, as a matter of fact. That's why everyone is racing around trying to get ready. We've got about half our normal staff, and Marco isn't even here."

That gave her pause. Any cousins of his might just be cousins of hers. They shared a great-great-grandfather from almost one hundred and fifty years back, and all the royals were tied together in one way or another. It might get a little sticky keeping up this masquerade if someone she knew showed up. But she would worry about that tomorrow.

"Where is your brother?" she asked him.

"He's in Dallas, I believe, looking over some princess he might be marrying."

"Oh." She knew about Marco, knew about the tragic loss of his young wife. "His story is so sad," she said quietly.

"True." Garth nodded. "Marco deserves happiness. I just hope he finds it in Dallas."

He didn't sound convinced that such a thing was possible. It was quite apparent to her that he was a cynic. He probably didn't believe in love. The question was, did she?

"And you have a younger sister, don't you?"

She had met Princess Karina at a luncheon celebrating the younger woman's graduation from college a few months before. Kari was a lovely young woman and she'd enjoyed talking to her. When she'd asked her about Garth, Kari had laughed once she'd mentioned the betrothal.

"Oh you poor thing," she'd said.

"It wasn't my idea," Tianna reminded her. "In fact, if I could think of a way to get out of it, I would."

Kari had laughed again. "You'll probably find a willing accomplice in my brother. I'm sure he will want to put off tying the knot as long as possible."

And that was when the plan was first born. If there was a chance that he wasn't any more eager for an arranged marriage than she was, she knew she had to follow up on it. So she'd come.

She'd met Garth. She'd found him just as appealing as everyone said he was. She was pretty sure he didn't care much about the betrothal on anything other than a convenience level. But would he be willing to give it up? At some point, she was going to have to confront him with that. Something told her that he wasn't going to be easy to deal with, no matter how smooth and charming he might seem right now. He was, after all, the second son of the king. And that certainly meant something in Nabotavian society. It all hinged on just what sort of man Prince Garth really was. But that was exactly what she'd come here to find out, wasn't it?

It was time to get back to the baby. She rose, making her excuses, and started for the door. Prince Garth followed her, reluctant to see her leave so soon. She was a beautiful woman and he was beginning to realize that he wanted her, wanted her badly, with a deep burning pulse such as he hadn't felt in years.

Maybe that's not it at all, he told himself a bit caustically. *Maybe I just need a drink.*

But he knew the truth. He wanted to kiss her. He wanted to undress her slowly and see her beautiful body in the lamplight and stroke and touch her until she cried out with need for him. That was what he wanted. All he had to do was figure out how to get it.

He was playing an old game. It was a great game. He'd played it often in past years. And he usually won. But something was different this time. Somehow the usual game didn't feel right with this one. Maybe he was going to have to step it up, take things to a higher level. Whatever that meant.

"Tianna," he said softly.

She turned in the doorway, looking up at him with

her beautiful green eyes rimmed with dark lashes. He touched her cheek and looked at her mouth. Desire was frothing inside him like champagne. One kiss ought to do the trick. Staring at her lips, he began to lower toward them.

"Oh," she said suddenly. "I forgot to tell you. I think I know what the baby's name is."

He drew back, annoyed. "What?" he said, not asking for the name, but asking why she would interrupt this wonderful moment with such mundane information.

She went on, earnestly. " I was looking at the little baby clothes she came in and there seems to be a name embroidered into the edging. Marika. Isn't that cute?" She smiled at him as though she expected him to be as delighted with it as she was. "Marika. An old-fashioned Nabotavian name, isn't it? I love it."

Garth choked. He felt the blood drain from his face.

"Good night," Tianna said cheerfully. Turning, she walked briskly down the corridor toward the nursery and he did nothing to stop her.

Marika. That was his mother's name, a nickname that was only used in the family. Marika. How could a stranger have known?

He turned back into the game room, shaken. Coincidence? It had to be. And yet...

A sense of impending doom slipped over him for a moment, but he shook it off. No. Facts were facts. That baby couldn't possibly be his.

Chapter Four

Tianna had a lot of time to think over her situation during the night. Baby Marika didn't seem to be real clear on the difference between the time to be awake and the time to be asleep. It wasn't that she was fussy. In fact, she didn't appear to have an ill-natured bone in her tiny little body. She was wide-awake, however, gurgling happy baby sounds and playing with her thumb.

Tianna's experience in putting a baby to sleep was limited but her attempts ran the gamut—walking, talking, rocking. She even tried a soft song or two, and was rewarded with big smiles, but no signs of sleep. Finally she gave up with a sigh and just stayed in the creaky old rocker, holding her, waiting for her eyelids to droop. And thinking over this strange day. As the hour grew later and the house grew quieter, the shadows seemed deeper and her thoughts grew more haunted.

Rocking the baby, she looked about the room. It was lovely with gingham curtains and an antique baby crib, along with the usual chests and baby-changing table. There was a handy sink, a tub for baby baths, and an attached bathroom. A simple adult bed sat along the wall, and that was where she would sleep— once she was allowed to! All in all, it was a comfortable situation.

But what in the world was she doing here? She'd come to discuss breaking her betrothal to Prince Garth, and ended up taking care of what was probably his illegitimate baby. What an unbelievable twist to her plans.

And yet, she knew she didn't have to stay. She didn't have to do this at all. All she had to do was announce who she was and they wouldn't allow her to act the nanny any longer. Which was exactly why she was staying quiet. There was something about this baby that tore at her heart. One look and she'd been hooked on the child.

She knew it was partly because Marika was a beautiful and good-natured baby. But surely there was more to it than that. Misty, faded memories of her own childhood had something to do with it. Seeing this baby left abandoned to the unknown called up barely remembered recollections of dark days, of loss and loneliness and reaching out for comfort, only to find a stranger holding her hand. Shuddering, she pushed the thoughts away and looked down into Marika's sweet face. Resolution steeled within her heart. This baby would not be frightened the way she had been if she had anything to do with it.

"And that, my *petit chou,* was how I became a nanny to the most beautiful baby in the world," she whispered softly as Marika cooed. Her long silky lashes were fluttering. Tianna held her breath. Yes! The eyes were closing. Finally, they were going to get some sleep.

The first rays of the sun appeared all too soon, and Marika met them with a loud crowing sound that signaled a new day was beginning. Tianna groaned as she tried to work up the same enthusiasm. Still groggy from lack of sleep, she rose and washed her face before cleaning and changing the tyke. Looking in the "nanny closet," she chose a tan rollneck cotton sweater and brown linen slacks. They fit just a bit larger than she would have liked, but all in all, she was lucky she had such a supply. Changing done, she wrapped Marika in a fresh blanket and carried her along on a trip to the kitchen.

She'd explored the floor where the nursery was the night before. The castle was beautiful, full of hardwood floors with Persian carpeting, velvet drapes and high-ceilinged rooms. Somehow the builders had managed to make it look as though it had been there for centuries.

Delicious smells wafted around her before she

opened the double doors to find the large kitchen buzzing with activity, even though it was barely dawn. Cook looked up and saw her right away, gesturing for her to come on in.

"Let's see her, then," she cried, holding out her flour-dusted arms. "How is the little angel this morning?"

Tianna handed her over and smiled as the other kitchen workers gathered around, oohing and aahing.

"She doesn't sleep much," she said as she turned to find the bottles and formula she knew Milla had stockpiled for her. "In fact, she was quite the night owl last night."

"Oh, she'll settle down once she's used to us," Cook said comfortably, then frowned and drew away when Milla offered to hold the baby. "You all get back to work now. We've got visitors coming this afternoon and we're way behind. I'll just hold on to this little darling while Tianna gets her breakfast ready. Shoo now, get on with you."

Her scolding didn't have much effect. Milla and the new pastry chef lingered along with Bridget, who'd stopped by for her morning coffee. They laughed softly over the baby, touching her little fingers, kissing the top of her downy head. It warmed Tianna to see them react that way to her. *Almost as though she were really my own,* she thought, then winced. That was the first time she'd let herself give form to a thought like that and she knew she would have to nip it in the bud. Marika was not hers and never would be. She had to guard against letting the child become too important to her.

"Do you know her name?" Cook asked, laughing as the baby grabbed for her finger.

"I believe it's Marika."

"Marika. That's a real old-fashioned Nabotavian name, isn't it? You don't hear it much these days." She smiled down at her armful. "Oh, I wish we could keep this one. She's a peach."

Tianna finished filling the bottle with warmed formula and took the baby from the cook, sitting down in a chair at the table to feed her. The servants bustled around her and she sat enjoying the smells and the small talk. But most of all, she enjoyed the whole experience of holding and feeding the baby. There was something about it that filled her with a delightful sense of happiness, and she really wasn't sure why.

As she finished up, she noticed that Janus had entered the kitchen and was preparing a tray. "Good morning," she said to him with a smile. "I certainly hope you have some luck today."

"Luck?" He looked at her blankly for a moment. "Oh, you mean in finding the child's mother? Oh, yes. Well, I plan to do a thorough investigation as soon as I can get away."

He stopped by, smiling down at Marika and touching her sweet cheek.

"Yes indeed," he said rather absently. "Yes indeed."

Tianna liked the way he interacted with the baby.

Something about the man gave her a feeling of security. He would find the mother, and probably very soon. He turned to go and she looked at Cook. Her stomach was definitely complaining it was being ignored.

"In what room is breakfast served?" she asked, looking forward to a proper meal.

Cook looked at her strangely. "Well, the nanny usually eats her breakfast here, with the staff, if she doesn't have it in the nursery," she said.

"Oh." Mentally, she kicked herself. She'd forgotten. She wasn't a princess here. She licked her lower lip, wondering how to repair the damage from her mistake.

But Janus saved her. He was just leaving himself, but he turned back and said, "I meant to tell you, Miss, His Highness is breakfasting in the morning room right now. He asked me to request that you join him as soon as you are free."

"Ah." She rose, trying to avoid meeting Cook's gaze. "I'll go to him right away," she said, then glanced at the woman and saw the disapproval she had known would be there. Cook seemed on the verge of stepping forward and giving her a piece of advice, but Tianna turned away. Advice was something she didn't need right now.

"Would you like me to hold the baby while you have your breakfast?" Milla offered.

"Oh no," Tianna said breezily as she started for the door. "I can have the prince hold her for me."

She had the impression of mouths gaping all around, but she didn't stay to see it. Janus led her to the morning room. He, at least, was smiling his approval.

Garth looked up and rose as she entered, and she favored him with a radiant smile in return. The room was lovely, shaped like an octagon and glassed in from floor to ceiling on four of those sides. The morning light flooded in, turning everything golden, including the prince's hair.

"Good morning," she said brightly.

He nodded, almost bowing. "Good morning to you," he said softly, and when she looked into his eyes, she saw a look that made her shiver. It seemed he liked what he saw. At least, until his gaze fell on the baby in her arms.

"Why don't you send her up to the nursery with Bridget?" he suggested. "You can't eat your breakfast with a baby on your shoulder."

"You're right," she said, noting that he had finished eating himself, and was relaxing with a cup of coffee. "But I have a better idea. I think you should hold her."

"Me?"

"You."

With no further ado, she plopped the baby in his arms and turned toward the sideboard to begin filling a plate with food. She watched him out of the corner of her eye. He stood thunderstruck for a moment, then appealed to his valet.

"Janus," he said. "You'd better take this thing quickly...."

"Sorry, sir," Janus said with a sly smile. "I'm just on my way to catch Homer before he takes the car in for repairs. You said you wanted to make sure he remembered to have that whistling sound checked."

"Oh. Of course." Garth stood where he was as Janus, his last hope, left the room. He held the baby as though it had something contagious. "Tianna, this is ridiculous," he said.

After looking things over and deciding he wasn't going to drop Marika, Tianna ignored him, humming a cheerful tune as she collected strips of bacon, mounds of scrambled egg, and pieces of buttered toast and arranged them neatly on her plate. Turning back to the table, she gave him a look of pure exasperation. "Oh, do sit down. She won't break."

He shot her a look that was meant to inflict pain, but he did as she suggested, sitting gingerly on the edge of his chair, trying to hold the baby without having her touch any part of him except his arms. Marika cooed and laughed into his face.

Tianna sat down and picked up her fork, watching him with growing amusement as he glowered down at the child. "What can you possibly have against a sweet little innocent baby?" she asked.

He glared at her, too. "Oh, I don't know. Let me count the ways. They cry, they smell, they make demands, they want to be carried around..."

"They smile, they laugh, they look so adorable..."

"They spit up milk."

"Well, sometimes, but…"

"No, I mean right now. Take her!" His voice held a note of horror.

"Oh!" Tianna jumped up, but instead of taking Marika herself, she threw a cloth diaper onto Garth's shoulder and propped the baby up against it in burping position. "There you go. Burp her."

"Burp her?" He said the word as though it were in a foreign tongue.

"Pat her back softly. Here. Like this."

She guided his hand. For just a moment, their gazes met, and suddenly it seemed that what they were doing together was awfully intimate. Tianna drew away and sat down. Looking rebellious, Garth went on patting Marika, awkwardly at first, but then more and more gracefully. Slowly, imperceptibly, he began to get his bearings.

Tianna ate her scrambled eggs, but her mind wasn't on food. She watched as Garth tried hard to do what the baby needed. He wasn't complaining any longer. He looked to be getting into it, though he was still frowning fiercely and making sure she knew this wasn't his idea of a good time. Marika's head was bobbing up and she was making enough noise to announce the fact that she didn't feel very comfortable. Another moment, and she might actually get fussy.

And then something magic happened. For just a moment, Prince Garth forgot himself, and he murmured a soft endearment against little Marika's downy head.

Tianna held her breath, staring down at her plate. What was that he'd said? Had she heard him whisper, "That's okay, sweetie?" She very carefully didn't look at him and kept the smile that threatened to shine from her face at bay. There! She heard it again. Putting her napkin to her lips, she allowed the smile to break through.

"What's so funny?" he asked, growling.

"Who's laughing?" she asked innocently.

He glared at her, but a huge burp burst from the tiny baby mouth, the sound echoing around the room, and suddenly they were all three laughing.

Bridget appeared in the doorway. "Cook told me to ask if you needed any help with the baby," she said, her eyes big as saucers at the sight of Garth holding the baby against his shoulder.

"Thank you, Bridget," Tianna said, taking charge as though it were the most natural thing in the world. "I think His Highness has done enough bonding with Marika for one morning. I would appreciate it if you would take her up to the nursery and sit with her until I come up. I have a few things to talk over with His Highness. I won't be long."

"Yes, Miss." Bridget did as she'd been told and Garth relaxed for the first time since Tianna had thrust the child in his arms.

That had been quite an adventure. No one had ever dumped a baby in his arms before. Actually, it hadn't turned out to be as monstrous as he'd thought it would. The sense of a small life in his hands had been strange, but rather appealing. Even so, he hoped he wouldn't have to repeat the experience and he was very glad Bridget had come to save the day.

"Now, back to business," Tianna was saying, clearing her plate to the side and leaning forward on her elbows, her green eyes bright with anticipation. "About finding Marika's mother."

Looking at her, he wondered how she could be so enchanting and so annoying at the same time. "Janus is handling that," he reminded her.

"I know. But I thought maybe we could go into town and ask around at some of the places where Nabotavians hang out...."

"Tianna." He took her warm, slender hand in his and held it. He could see how important this was to her. It shone from her face, resonated in her voice. He could almost feel it in the pulse at her wrist. "Why do you care so much about this baby?" he asked, searching her eyes for the answer.

She blinked, took in a ragged breath and pulled her hand from his, reaching for her glass of orange juice to mask the move. "The question really is, why do you care so little?" she countered, taking a sip.

That was an easy one.

"Because that baby isn't mine."

He'd been thrown for a few minutes the night before when he'd heard the baby's name. It still seemed an odd coincidence. But Marika had once been a common and endearing name in Nabotavia. It wasn't all that unusual. Just an accident. That was all.

"How can you be so sure?" she asked him.

"Because I know. What more can I say?"

She shook her head. His gaze followed the movement of her silky hair, the way it brushed against her slim neck, the way one deep wave curled around her chin line, and he felt a deep response that made him wince. He couldn't believe he was reacting to something so ordinary. But then, it wasn't really the hair, was it? It was the totality of the woman. He wanted her. Frowning hard, he suppressed the thought. This was no time to get bogged down in plain old garden-variety lust. He could see that she was making an effort to get through to him, that she was about to ask something she knew wasn't going to be well received. So he waited, giving her a chance.

She twisted her hands together and stared down at her entwined fingers. "Are you trying to tell me it would be impossible?" she asked hesitantly.

He knew what she was getting at, but he didn't make it any easier for her. "I would say so, yes."

Her lashes fluttered. "Are you...unable to have children?"

She made herself look him in the eye as she asked it, and he almost laughed at how brave she was being. There was no need for her uneasiness. He wasn't offended by the query. Still, he couldn't help but tease her a little.

"Tianna, I'm surprised at you. That's a rather personal question."

The flush that flooded her cheeks only made her

more beautiful. "The entire topic is personal," she said stoutly, nonetheless. "Very personal. And I only ask because…"

"I know, I know. Your whole concern is for the good of the child."

She took a deep breath and looked relieved. "Yes. And you didn't answer the question."

He looked at her and laughed. "Come on," he said, rising and putting out his hand to take hers. "Let's go out on the terrace. I want to have a cigarette."

"You shouldn't smoke," she said automatically, but she rose and let him take her hand, leading her out through the French doors onto the wide terrace that overlooked the rolling lawns which swept out from the castle. Down below was a series of ponds connected with small waterfalls. They stood together at the railing, looking down at the grounds. The beauty of the stark horizon peaks, so different from the lush forest-covered mountains of her Washington State home, was beginning to grow on her. The sky seemed so big. And the rain the day before had left everything feeling so clean. For a few minutes, she took it all in, breathing the fresh air, letting her gaze travel over the landscape—and wishing she had brought along a camera or two. And Garth stood silently beside her, a presence she couldn't ignore. The more she avoided looking at him, the more he seemed to loom in her awareness, touching all her senses. Maybe it would be better to face him. She turned with dogged determination.

"You still haven't answered my question," she said.

He chuckled. "Don't worry about my ability to carry on the name, Tianna," he said. "As far as I know, there are no problems along those lines." He turned, leaning on the railing, looking at her in a way that made her think of candlelight and the scent of gardenias. "There is no way I can prove it to you, but I know I didn't father that baby."

She started to say something, then cut it back and bit her lip. He could see that she was searching for some way to reach him. How was he going to convince her that it was no use?

She avoided his gaze again, looking out toward the mountains. "Maybe you just don't remember," she suggested. "Maybe you were drinking and…"

"I'm not that much of a drinker, Tianna." He said it smoothly, but she could detect the underlying annoyance that was growing. "In fact, the other night was the first time in a long time…." He hesitated, hating the way it sounded like making excuses. "Believe what you want to believe," he said shortly. "She's not my baby. And I don't plan to have a child outside of wedlock. It doesn't do anybody any good, from what I've seen."

"And you've never been married," she said, stating the obvious as though she had to get it nailed down.

"You know I've never been married." He shoved his hands into his pockets and gazed at her speculatively. "Of course, I *am* betrothed."

"Betrothed?" She turned slowly to face him, her eyes wary, her cheeks blushing more than ever.

He frowned, not sure why he'd brought it up. It wasn't something he thought about much. Somehow it had popped into his head and he'd expressed it out loud.

"A technicality, really," he added quickly. "A hangover from the old days. I shouldn't have mentioned it."

She was looking determined again. He'd never known a woman who was so bad at hiding her feelings. And for some strange reason, he found that absolutely charming, even though her feelings so often seemed to run against him.

"No, I'm glad you did," she said, looking at him obliquely. "I find this quite interesting." She turned so that she could see directly into his eyes. "Who's the lucky girl?"

"A minor princess." He shrugged it off as though it were hardly worth mentioning. "From West Nabotavia. I doubt you've heard of her."

"A minor princess." Tianna had to turn away so that he wouldn't see the fire in her eyes. *Minor, eh?* "Fascinating. Do you have a wedding planned?"

"Uh...no, not really." He wished he'd never brought it up. "It's sort of just looming in my future somewhere. I think she's too young or something." He reached into his pocket for his cigarettes. He didn't know why an uneasy feeling was beginning to nag at him. There was something about this subject that felt strangely awkward at the moment.

"So you're in no hurry to marry." She turned, her back and elbows on the railing, and looked at him almost challengingly.

"Are you kidding?" His laugh was utterly genuine. "Do I look like marriage material to you?"

She put her head to the side and pretended to look him over. "Oh, I don't know. A good wife might be able to make a man out of you."

One dark eyebrow rose. This had to be the first time in many years anyone had implied he lacked manhood.

She waited a beat before amplifying, enjoying his surprised response. "A *mature* man," she said at last. "A man who is ready to take on life instead of hiding from it."

"Hiding from it?" he said, and now he was finally offended. "Listen Tianna Rose, I've seen more of life than you'll ever dream of."

"Really?" She sniffed. "Too bad you don't seem to have learned much from all your experience." Her eyes flashed. "For instance, don't you know that those things will kill you?" She nodded at the pack of cigarettes he held in his hand.

He looked at them, then back at her with a cynical smile. "No, they won't. I'm quitting. This is my last pack."

"Hmm." She'd heard that one before. Her father had smoked for years. The whole family had celebrated once he'd quit for good.

"*I'm* from West Nabotavia, you know," she said, not sure why she was pushing it. She really didn't want him to realize who she was. Not yet. But at the same time, the fact that he thought so lightly of her...or of the "minor" princess he was betrothed to...drove her crazy.

"Ah, a Westie," he said, using the vaguely patronizing word regular Nabotavians often used for her sort.

"No, not a Westie," she said icily. "A White Rose Nabotavian."

"Yes." His smile was so darn dazzling. "If they all look like you, maybe she won't be so bad."

She choked and looked away. Talk about a double-edged compliment. It was too bad she couldn't show him just how angry this talk was making her. "I guess you aren't expecting much?"

"No, from what I hear, she's a real homebody. They say she's quiet, though forthright with her opinions, but would rather read than go to parties." He gave her a comical look as he tore open the package in his hand. "Now does that sound like any sort of match for me?"

Oh, the conceit of the man! She itched to wring his neck. "So you've asked around about her, then?" she said carefully, seething inside.

Setting the pack of cigarettes on the polished wood railing, he began to search his pockets for a light. "Actually, Marco was trying to get me to go visit her. He told me she is supposed to be 'very pretty.' Now, when Marco says 'very pretty' in that tone of voice, it's time to head for the hills. I have no doubt she's plain as toast. And just as dull.''

Oh! She wanted to throw something at him. The urge was impossibly strong. She looked around for something, anything, to get her hands on, and her gaze fell on the pack of cigarettes sitting on the railing while he searched his pockets for his lighter. Slowly, deliberately, she reached out and flicked the pack with her forefinger. It shot through the air and went sailing down into the pond below. She leaned over the railing, staring after it, feeling triumphant.

''Tianna,'' he said, looking at her strangely.

''Oops,'' she responded, still watching the pack float among the lily pads. ''It was an accident. I'm so sorry.''

''No, you're not.'' He stared at her, fascinated. ''You did that on purpose.''

Looking up, she met his eyes. She lifted her chin and gazed at him defiantly. ''I did not.''

''Yes, you did,'' he said with a half laugh. ''You very carefully knocked my cigarettes down into the water. You little devil!''

She began to back away, her eyes very large. ''I said I was sorry.''

''But you're not sorry at all.'' For every step she took backward, he took one toward her, his eyes filled with amusement and resolve. ''And I'm going to have to exact some kind of retribution. Just for my own self-respect, you understand.''

Beginning to worry about just what he might have

in mind, she shot him a blazing look and turned on her heel. "I'm going in," she said breezily. "I'll see you later."

But she hardly got two steps before he'd cornered her against the wall.

"You're not going anywhere until we settle this," he told her, his eyes sparkling with the fun of the chase. "Now I've got you right where I want you." With both hands flat on the stone wall, he had her effectively trapped and he leaned closer. "What should I do to get my revenge?" he asked musingly.

"Your Highness, let me go this instant," she ordered, with somewhat more spirit than an employee would normally use toward her employer.

"Oh no. I can't do that."

"Yes, you can. I'm…I'm sorry about the cigarettes. I'll buy you another pack."

"There are some things," he said in a very low and provocative voice, "more addictive than smoking."

"Are there?" she said breathlessly, then shook herself. "I mean, let me go!"

He leaned closer, so close that she could smell his crisp, clean scent, so close that she thought she could feel the heat rising from the open neck of his cotton shirt. "Say 'uncle,'" he said softly, his gaze caressing her face in a way that was almost tactile.

"Uncle?"

He shrugged lightly, his breath tickling the tender skin below her ear. "It's traditional. You've got to say it to be set free."

Well, then… "Uncle! Uncle!"

"Hmm." Leaning even closer, he didn't show any signs of relenting. He dropped a small kiss on the cord of her neck, giving her a delicious shiver, then drew back enough to see her face. "No, try 'strawberries.'"

"What for?"

He smiled. "To put your lips in a kissable position."

"What?" she cried, outraged.

"That'll do."

She put her hands up to stop him and found her fingers curling against his muscular chest. She raised her chin to show defiance, but quickly realized it seemed more like acquiescence. And then his warm mouth was meeting hers and her brain went into a snow pattern.

She hadn't meant to let this happen, but once it did, she found herself powerless to stop it. And then she didn't want to stop it. She'd been kissed before, and she'd definitely liked it. But this was something else again. Instead of awkward groping and noses getting in the way, this felt as though the two of them had been specially made to go together. Their bodies seemed to fit, their arms were in exactly the right place, and their lips touched, and then clung together, fused together, causing their mouths to melt together, all smooth, liquid heat and sweet, intoxicating taste, with just a touch of exotic spice to add excitement.

She loved this. She wanted more, and she reached hungrily for all she could get, yearning toward him.

His arms tightened around her, held her so close, she could barely breathe. But she didn't care. She was living in the moment, and all she needed in her lungs, in her life, in her heart, was this wonderful strong man.

Garth wasn't quite as blind to all sensible intelligence as she was, but it was darn close. It had been a long time since he'd lost his head over a woman. In fact, he would have had a hard time thinking of an instance where it might have happened before. In all his romantic adventures, there always seemed to be a part of him that stood aloof, watching it all with a cynical air, waiting for the pretending to be over, waiting for the masks to come off and the real human beneath the veneer to emerge and ruin everything. He'd never really been in love. He didn't think much of the concept. In his mind, love was an excuse people made for doing something foolish. Love meant losing control. And he always had to keep control.

Still, something about this warm and wonderful woman was making his head spin. She tasted so good, and her body seemed to be made for his. This simple kiss was giving him more gratification and satisfaction than many a full half hour of sexual interaction ever had in the past. For just a moment, he lost himself in the magic of her copper-colored hair, the smell of her buttery skin, the feel of her full breasts against him, the provocative way her hips seemed to invite him to linger, the taste of her hot, willing mouth. It wasn't until a phrase drifted into his mind that he regained control of his senses.

Do you realize you are kissing the nanny?

He reacted almost as though someone had spoken it out loud, his head jerking back, his body pushing away from hers. And he stared at her.

She stared right back. ''Wow,'' she said raggedly, her heart beating wildly, her breath coming in shaky gulps. ''We'd better not do that again.''

He stared at her a moment longer, and then he began to laugh. She ducked around him and made her escape. When she reached the French doors, she looked back. He was still laughing. She turned and made her way back to the nursery, her heart pounding.

She didn't know if she was insulted or pleased. Her hands were still shaking. That kiss had really thrown her for a loop. What exactly was going on here? Stopping outside the door to the nursery, she took a deep breath and steadied herself. She had to keep her focus. Baby Marika was what mattered. Kisses on the terrace could only cloud the picture. If she didn't watch out, she might find herself falling for the very man she'd come here to get rid of!

Chapter Five

"Don't you think it would be a good idea to get the police involved? At least they might be able to canvas the neighborhood and ask for any suspicious sightings."

Tianna watched as Janus picked up Marika and held her above his head, murmuring nonsense noises at her. The baby gurgled and wiggled with happiness. It was wonderful to see this man with this baby. But it did give her a pang to think the man holding her should probably have been Garth.

"No police," Janus said in a tone that brooked no argument as he swung the baby down again and held her in his arms. He'd just come back from a trip into Flagstaff but had not been lucky in finding out anything much. He had collected a few contacts he planned to call, though, organizations and individuals who he thought might be able to help. Tianna wasn't exactly thrilled with how slowly this seemed to be going.

"What do you have against the police?" she asked, frowning.

"No police," he repeated, putting Marika back down in her bed. "We don't deal with the police here. Leave it at that."

She wanted to argue with him, but held her tongue for now.

"Another thing," she said. "I'd like to set her up with a doctor's appointment. She seems to be fine, but I do think a basic checkup is in order."

He nodded. "I will call the pediatrician Marco uses for his children. I'll take care of that right away."

She sighed. Another item marked off her list. But she still had a feeling she was leaving something out. She wished she had more experience.

"I'm going to give her the first full-fledged bath she's had since she came," she told him, nodding at the little baby tub she'd set up on the counter. "And I'm a little nervous about it."

He smiled. "You'll do fine. Just don't leave her alone for even one second."

"Oh no, of course not."

He seemed to know so much about babies. It made her smile. He was reassuring. And she supposed he was doing everything he could to locate Marika's mother. She wanted to jump in and help, but he probably knew best. She would leave it to him for the time being.

Still, time was running out. She couldn't stay here forever, pretending to be a nanny. She'd called her sister, Janni, who knew all about her trip, and told her things had changed and that she wouldn't be back home for a few more days than she'd planned.

"You'll cover for me with the parentals, won't you?"

"Of course. You covered for me often enough in the old days."

"True." Tianna answered ruefully, knowing it might not have been the best thing she ever did for her sister.

"But have you broken the engagement yet?" Janni had asked her.

"No, not yet. I have to get this baby taken care of first." She'd sighed. "Once Prince Garth knows why I'm really here, he'll want to get rid of me as quickly as possible. And I won't be able to do a thing for the baby."

"So tell me, what's he like?"

Tianna opened her mouth but she couldn't seem to get out a statement. "Uh…"

"I heard he's very handsome. True or not?"

"Oh, uh…yes, that's certainly true."

There was a pause, then Janni gave a little cry.

"Ohmigod. You're falling for him, aren't you?"

"No!"

"You are! Oh, this is too rich!"

"I am not. I'm getting out of this betrothal if it kills me."

"Sure, but just not quite yet," Janni noted with a sisterly laugh.

Tianna wasn't sure why sisters who could be so helpful and loving could also be so darn irritating, but it really was true. She told her sister goodbye rather icily and went back to watching Marika. About an hour later, Janus had arrived to give her his disappointing progress report. And here they were.

"Janus, what will happen if we can't find the mother?"

Janus looked almost as worried about that prospect as she did herself. "It will have to be the Nabotavian orphanage I suppose," he said. "I don't know of any alternative."

No, she thought, looking down at the antique crib. A chill skittered down her spine. *No. Anything but that.*

"Janus, tell me the truth. Do you think she's the prince's child?"

He looked shocked and she realized he might not know all the details that would make her say such a thing. But there was no time to linger over protocol.

"I know you think that an impertinent question," she said quickly. "But I am really very attached to this baby and I'm trying to do what's best for her. There has been an allegation that Prince Garth is her father, and I'm only asking if you think that might be possible."

Janus looked uncomfortable. He cleared his throat and stood back, folding his arms across his chest.

"I don't know, Miss," he said at last. "But I do want to say this. Prince Garth plays the part of the libertine, but it is mostly just that—an act. There was a time, a few years ago, when he got into the wild life, the international jet set scene, a little too heavily. But these days, you'll rarely find him drinking anything more than a simple glass of wine with dinner. And as for the women…" He shrugged in a very continental manner. "Those have been few and far between as well, for the last three years at least." He looked at her earnestly. "I've known him all his life and this I can say without hesitation. He's a very decent man. I know that doesn't answer your question, but it is the best I can do."

Tianna bit her lip and sighed. "Thank you, Janus. You've answered my question quite nicely."

And he had, really. If Prince Garth insisted he wasn't the father, maybe it was time to stop accusing him. Because her instincts were telling her Janus was right. The prince was a good man, despite all that others might think. If he thought he was responsible for this child's existence, she was beginning to believe he would assume the burden as a matter of course, regardless of how he felt about the issue.

She frowned, wondering if these thoughts she was having were tainted by his having kissed her. Was she giving him all this credit because he deserved it—or because she was, as Janni had screeched at her, "falling for him." Who knew?

Prince Garth rapped on the nursery door. He didn't know why he was here. He had better places to be, more important things to do. He'd spent the past few hours completely unable to concentrate on his work and he had a lot of correspondence that needed answering, phone calls to return. In other words, he had work to do. And yet, here he was.

The door opened and he was surprised to find his valet visiting. He glanced from one face to the other. Looking into Tianna's emerald eyes, he caught a flash of wordless communication. They both were remembering what had happened on the terrace. Something had changed between them and they both knew it. Still, she was looking at him expectantly, wondering why he was here.

And why not? He was wondering, too. Why the hell *was* he here? He ran a hand distractedly through his hair and frowned.

"I…uh…thought I'd come see how the baby is," he said, knowing that sounded transparently feeble. But it elicited such a look of shining happiness from Tianna, he immediately felt better about it. In fact, Janus looked pretty pleased, too.

But at the same time, the valet was beating a hasty retreat.

"If you have no need of me, Your Highness, I am anxious to make a few phone calls before it gets too late.'' He gestured toward where Marika lay. ''They have to do with the parentage of the child.''

''Of course. Do what you must.''

Janus hesitated. ''Miss Rose, you might see if the prince will help you with the baby's bath, if you are still feeling nervous about it.''

''Good idea,'' she murmured.

Janus gave his employer a significant look and left the room.

The prince nodded to him, but his attention was filled with his sense of Tianna's presence. Meeting her gaze again, he caught a flash of apprehension. Yes, they were going to be alone together once more. He felt the same quiver of excitement that he could see in her. This was dangerous stuff and he wasn't sure why he was tempting fate.

She turned to the baby, bending over the crib, in an obvious move to avoid looking at him. ''Look, Marika,'' she said softly. ''Look who's come to see you.''

He bent over the crib, too, as it seemed to be expected. ''Hi,'' he said. The baby turned her sleepy blue eyes toward him and stared. ''Hi, Marika.''

Marika. That name. Suddenly he was transported back over twenty years, and his mother was the Marika he was seeing, not this baby.

''Marika,'' his father was saying, reaching for his beautiful wife. ''Darling one, I promise we will all be safe. Trust me.''

His mother's arms wrapped around him and held him close, even as his father pulled them both closer

into his protective embrace. He could smell the rose
scent his mother wore, feel her kiss on his cheek. They
would all be safe. His father had promised.

But his father couldn't keep that promise. Within
days, both his parents were dead. The old, familiar
sense of loss choked him, but anger rose quickly to
take its place, burning in his chest. Reflexively, his
hands clenched into fists.

"What's the matter?" Tianna asked.

He looked at her, startled back to the here and now.
"Nothing," he said, shaking his head.

"There was something," she insisted, putting her
hand on his arm. "Are you in pain? Is something
wrong?"

Surprised, he looked deep into the misty depths of
her eyes. He saw real concern there. This wasn't
merely a social nicety. She cared. That touched a
chord in his soul, resonating inside him and for just a
moment, he had a lump in his throat.

And then he wanted to kiss her again. It was getting
so that he couldn't look at her without wanting to
touch her. He made a move toward her, and almost
imperceptibly, she shook her head, her eyes huge.

He stopped. She was right, of course. It would be
skating a bit close to the edge to risk holding her in
his arms with a bed so close by. He really ought to
get out of here and back to his work.

She watched his face, wondering what he was thinking. Marika babbled something babylike and he turned
to look down at her. Almost against his will, she saw

a smile begin to curl his wide mouth, and he put his hand into range, forefinger extended. Marika gurgled and reached for it, her tiny fingers trying to grab his finger, her little perfect mouth open with her effort.

He laughed and Tianna came up next to him, looking down as well, watching the prince play with the baby. Just the day before he'd refused to even think of holding her, so some progress was being made. That gave her the nerve to ask him the same question she'd asked Janus.

"Prince Garth, tell me this. If we can't find the mother and the final determination is that you had nothing to do with this baby, what will become of her?"

"She'll go to the Nabotavian orphanage, of course," he said without hesitation. "That's what it's there for."

She sighed. They'd both said the same thing. That made it just about the final word, and it worried her. For just a moment, she had wild thoughts of trying to adopt Marika herself. But she knew that wouldn't work. She was going to Chicago to start a career in photography. She couldn't take a baby along. It wouldn't be fair to the baby.

Maybe her sister…? But no. Janni had her hands full with her own baby as it was, and raising her child at home with their parents was no picnic. Her mother and father were wonderful and loving in many ways, but they did disapprove of things Janni had done and they weren't afraid to let it show on occasion.

"After her bath, I'm going to put her in a play suit and take her outside for a ride around in the stroller," she told him. "Would you like to come with us?"

"I'm sorely tempted," he admitted. "But my cousins should be arriving very soon. I've got some work I must get done before they get here."

"Oh. Of course." She'd forgotten about the cousins, though she'd heard the upstairs maids rushing about freshening rooms all day. She was going to have to be careful once they got here. "How many are coming?"

He shrugged. "They can't seem to go anywhere without bringing all their friends along, so it's liable to be a large group. They are only staying the night. They're off in the morning to Gallup, New Mexico to see the Native American dances and buy some turquoise."

"Good," she said. "I guess I'd better get our little outdoor excursion underway so that we can get back inside and out of sight before they arrive."

He started to ask her why she felt she had to be out of sight, but Marika, feeling neglected, let out a piercing squeal that had them both laughing at her, and he let it go. Tianna began filling the baby tub for Marika's bath, while the prince found himself playing peekaboo—and only feeling slightly ridiculous.

"One thing's for sure," he said to Tianna. "Whoever wandered in and left Marika in the yard must have been heartbroken to do it. This is one adorable baby."

Tianna nodded, pleased he could finally admit it. "Speaking of wandering in," she said. "Have you done anything about the security on this property?"

He turned to look at her. "Pushy, aren't you?" he noted. "Don't worry about it. We've got it under control."

She bit her tongue and held back the sharp retort she had ready for that statement. "Have you ever had any sort of real problem with people breaking in?" she asked instead.

"Nothing serious. Not here at any rate." He helped her move the tub full of warm water onto the counter where she would be using it.

"My sister Kari, who lives with our aunt and uncle in Beverly Hills, has to be protected at all times. There have been a few attempts to kidnap her. But no one has tried to kidnap me or my brother as yet. They wouldn't dare. They know they would never get away with it."

Tianna stopped and looked at him, suddenly chilled. After all, the history of his family was rife with tragedy. "Kidnapping might not be the only way to get to you. What if they only want to…to kill you?"

"True. That's a possibility. But no such attempt has been made, so…" He shrugged.

"That doesn't mean it might not happen."

She thought about what her father had told her about the background of the rebellion in Nabotavia. Her own branch of the family was never under threat. They didn't have much real power. So they had been able to move into a nice neighborhood in the Seattle area and live like anyone else, keeping a low profile and quietly going on about their lives. But the Roseanovas were different. They were the ones who'd had all the power, and therefore all the danger. Suddenly she was alarmed that Garth wasn't taking better precautions.

"I don't care about you, personally," she said quickly to make sure he didn't get the wrong idea. "I care about Nabotavia, especially in this critical time."

And that was true, she realized suddenly, and it surprised her. How strange. She hadn't ever thought so much about being Nabotavian as she had since she'd arrived in this place. Knowing the prince was giving her a whole new perspective on her background.

"Of course," he said, but amusement was shining in his eyes.

She couldn't help but smile back at him. "Hand me the washrags, please," she said to change the subject.

He turned toward where she'd pointed and located the items she'd asked for, but something caught his eye before he'd completed the move toward them. Reaching around the changing table, he pulled a crumpled piece of cloth out of a pile of laundry and frowned at it.

"Tianna," he said carefully. "Where did this come from?"

"What? Oh, that cloth? It was with the baby. It was inside the baby's blanket, sort of as a liner. Why?"

He spread it out, flattening it with his hands.

"Look," he said, drawing her attention to the pattern woven into the damask cloth. "It's the family crest. The Red Rose crest." He looked at her strangely. "We used to have this sort of thing when I was a child. No one was allowed to use this except the royal family in those days."

She met his gaze. "How strange," she murmured, not sure what he was thinking.

He nodded. "Too strange." His voice was almost angry now. "Dammit. I wish Marika's mother would show up. I'm getting tired of all the mystery surrounding this baby."

Tianna found it rather reassuring that he was beginning to let the situation touch him a little more deeply. She wanted to talk to him about his reactions, but his cell phone rang.

"Can you handle the bath by yourself?" he asked, grimacing. "I've got a long distance call from Nabotavia. I'm going to have to go down to the study to take it."

"Go ahead," she told him. "We'll be fine."

He looked at her and for one fleeting moment, she thought he might lean forward and drop a kiss on her lips before he left. But the moment passed and he only gave her a smile before he went out the door.

She sighed. Finding the cloth seemed to bother him a lot and Tianna wasn't sure why. Had it shaken his faith in his own position?

But she didn't have a lot of time to think about that. The bath loomed, a little scary, but soon underway, and going well. Marika splashed in the water, enjoying it just as she seemed to enjoy everything in life. And once Tianna had pulled all her clothes off, she discovered something she hadn't noticed before. Just over her heart, on her chubby little baby chest, there was a wine-red birthmark about an inch and a half long. And for the life of her, Tianna couldn't shake the opinion that it looked very much like a rosebud just beginning to open.

"How very appropriate," she told the wet and wiggly baby. "You see, Marika? You were made for this family."

The cousins arrived sooner than expected and caught Tianna as she was coming in from her walk with Marika. She had just unstrapped the little girl from the huge stroller and taken her up in her arms when two long black limousines drove up to the front door. There was no time to run. Before she fully realized what was happening, the drivers were out and opening the car doors. Two footmen from the castle came out to carry in the luggage, and suddenly women of all ages and all shapes and sizes were leaving the cars and descending on the castle—"Like flies on a week-old pizza," Tianna muttered to herself, using one of her brother's favorite phrases.

Oh well, maybe they would all be strangers. It was quite likely, after all. The members of her family weren't exactly a bunch of social butterflies. She would have to hold her ground and hope for the best.

As she stood between the cars and the castle entry-way, the entire entourage was coming straight for her when she suddenly realized she knew one of the women. She clutched the baby tightly to her chest and gulped, her heart beating a bit faster. The jig was up, she supposed. Her charade would be exposed. The third woman coming her way was the Duchess of Tab-liva, an old friend of her mother's. She'd been taken to visit her once years before, at her beautiful bay-view apartment in San Francisco. She remembered it well, mostly because of that stunning view. Tea had been served on the terrace and they had watched fog roll in across the water while the sun retreated into the mist. She'd thought at the time that was one appealing thing about being royalty—you did tend to get good housing.

She had an urge to turn and dash out of the way and hope for the best, but it was too late. They were marching right past her. She pasted a smile on her face and lifted her chin, determined to take her medicine bravely. The first woman brushed on by without a glance. The second woman seemed to see right through her. And the duchess, the woman her mother counted as one of her dear friends, let her glance touch briefly on the baby, then made a face, as though children didn't please her, and walked on past without a sign of any recognition at all.

Tianna stood where she was, stunned. They were passing her as though she were a potted plant. Anxiety gave way to annoyance, and she began to glare at the remaining women as they hurried past her. No one noticed. Not one of them met her gaze. Even two beautiful young ones who brought up the rear.

She couldn't believe it. Most of these women were royals or close to it. How could they be so unutterably rude? She certainly wasn't used to being ignored this way. How dared they?

And then it came to her.

They treated you like the servant you're pretending to be. What on earth do you expect?

She stayed where she was for a few more minutes, digesting what had just happened, rummaging through her memories, trying to recall if she'd treated servants as she'd just been treated. And she couldn't remember. Was that because she hadn't done it? Or because doing it came so naturally, she didn't retain the incidents? She wasn't sure. But she *was* sure she would be more aware in the future. Being ignored didn't feel good. She hated it.

Two footmen who'd travelled with the group were coming up to the stairs now, and she looked at them. They weren't ignoring her at any rate. The older ducked his head and reined in a smile, but the younger one, a short but cocky-looking fellow with a snub nose and a wide grin gave her a wink.

"Hey, honey, meet ya' later in the kitchen?" he suggested hopefully as he walked past her.

She drew herself up, astounded, even though she now realized he thought she was a nanny and was just treating her accordingly. Her outrage dimmed and she gave him a toss of her head rather than the tongue-lashing that first came to mind.

Obviously, she was going to have to deal with the way she was treated, and the way she was treated was molded very much by the image she projected to the world.

"Come on, sweetheart," she told Marika, leaving the stroller behind as she started for the castle herself. "Let's go in and work on our attitudes."

Chapter Six

The visitors seemed to have turned the castle upside down. There was constant commotion, people rushing down hallways, doors banging, voices calling out. An entirely different atmosphere settled over the house.

Tianna sat restlessly in the nursery, feeling like a caged animal.

"A bunny in a box," she told Marika reassuringly. "Nothing too scary for little girls."

Marika pursed her lips and seemed to be considering what her nanny had said, making Tianna laugh.

She wanted to go out and see what was going on but she knew that would be too risky. So she sat, playing with Marika while she was awake, pacing the floor when the baby was asleep, wishing she had a good book with her. Late in the afternoon, things seemed to settle down and she assumed they had all gathered in the garden for tea—earlier she had seen the footmen setting up tables. Taking her chance, she picked up Marika and headed for the kitchen to restock the baby's food supply.

As usual, the kitchen staff was delighted to see Marika, even though they were busy serving little sandwiches and tarts on silver plates.

"I went into town and got you that baby food you wanted," Milla told Tianna after she'd given the baby a hug. She produced tiny jars of swirled peas and banana cereal.

"Oh good. I really do want to try some of the cereal with her. I'd say she's old enough."

Milla put her head to the side. "How old would you say she is?" she ventured.

"About four months." She shifted the baby so she could take hold of the bag full of baby food. "Does anyone know where Janus is?" she asked. She was anxiously waiting to hear his latest report on how the search was going. But no one seemed to have an answer.

"If you see him, please tell him I'd like to talk to him," she told them all. "I guess I'll get out of your way for now."

She started back toward the nursery but the laughter of the garden party drew her to a bank of tall windows on a landing where she could look down on the group. There were four or five decorated tables set up beneath the arbor. It looked like everyone was having a good time. She wondered who they all were, and where

Prince Garth was. Craning her neck, she began looking for him among the throng.

"Want to join the party?"

She whirled, and found the prince leaning against a doorjamb, smiling at her. He looked tall and elegant in a casual suit, the shirt open at the neck. Her breath caught in her throat for just a moment.

"You look like a child who wasn't invited to the birthday party," he continued. "Why don't you come on down and join in?"

She shook her head, marveling at the charge of excitement that seemed to sweep through her system at the sight of him. This wasn't good. "No thanks," she said quickly. "I've got…things to do."

"Ah, the ubiquitous 'things to do.' They're always first on my list."

"Yes." She avoided his mocking gaze and glanced back out the window, though she was turning to go.

"Tell you what," he said, straightening. "I'll have someone set up a little table for you here at the window. You can watch the group and have some afternoon tea of your own right here."

Suddenly that sounded like a lot of fun. She knew how good those little finger sandwiches had looked in the kitchen. She could symbolically join in and yet not risk identification from the duchess.

"What a good idea," she told him radiantly.

Pulling out his cell phone, he made a quick call to the butler's pantry to make arrangements. She waited for him to put the phone away, then put Marika in his arms, startling him.

"Here, hold her for a moment, and I'll run these things back to the room and get her sling chair. I'll only be a second."

Not waiting to see if he was really willing to baby-sit, she turned and hurried toward the room, humming as she went.

The prince looked down at Marika. She smiled up at him. He had to laugh. He was dead sure she couldn't be his, despite the name business and that royal cloth she'd come in, but once he had a baby, he would be darn lucky if she turned out half as cute and personable as this one.

Tianna was back in a flash, just as she'd promised, and by then, he was holding the baby as though he were an old hand at it.

Which, in fact, turned out to be a lot closer to the truth than either of them had imagined. Cook arrived with a tray of goodies just as a footman showed up with the table. The good woman took one look at Prince Garth and began to laugh.

"I declare, that does take me back some. You always were so good with babies."

Prince Garth looked at her as though she'd gone demented. "What are you talking about?"

"Don't you remember? When you were a young 'un. You used to carry your little sister Kari around like a rag doll. You wouldn't let anyone else near her." She set down her tray and began to serve tea.

"He was quite the protective brother, you know. I think all that horror of fleeing the country and our beloved king and queen...well, you know the story. It made our little prince want to protect what he had left. At least that was the way we saw it at the time." She shook her head, her eyes seeing a past twenty years back. "They were so young for so much heartbreak," she murmured. "Well, you enjoy the eats, now. I think you'll like what I've brought you."

Cook smiled at the picture the prince made holding Marika, but Tianna noticed she had to wipe her eyes as she turned to go. It was interesting how much more immediate the ties to Nabotavia were in this household than they had been in the atmosphere she had grown up in. It was as though the past were only yesterday, and everyone made reference to it all the time. In her family, the past was the past, and they all tried to push it into the background as they looked forward to a future without all the heartache and pain. Her own trauma from those days was never mentioned—as though it could somehow be erased by ignoring it.

"Thank you so much," she said to the prince as she took the baby into her own arms and put her in the sling seat. She noticed there were two chairs at the little table, but it still surprised her when the prince sat down with her.

"Shouldn't you be entertaining your guests?" she asked him, taking a bite from a watercress sandwich and rolling her eyes with the deliciousness of it all.

"They entertain themselves quite nicely." He

watched her, seeming to enjoy what he was looking at, making her feel a bit self-conscious.

"But they came to visit you," she reminded him.

He leaned back sideways in his char, throwing one arm over the back of it. "In a manner of speaking. Actually, they came to take charge of my life. And since I'm not about to let that happen, they will be much happier talking about it among themselves." His eyes shone with suppressed amusement. "Once I get into the conversation, I'm afraid there will be much rending of garments and gnashing of teeth. Tears will be shed. Oaths will be spoken."

She was laughing and trying not to. But something about the way he gave his narrative struck her as funny and she couldn't help it. "And what are they trying to get you to do that you are so determined to resist?" she asked him.

"Take a look for yourself." Looking down at the assembled guests, he nodded toward the dark-haired of the two pretty young ladies Tianna had noticed when the group had arrived. "There she is," he said. "What do you think of her?"

Tianna sighed, popping a salmon tidbit into her mouth. "She looks so young."

"She *is* young." His brows furled as he pretended to consider that concept. "But young can be good. You can train them when you get them young. Older women are already so opinionated." He cocked an eyebrow, teasingly. "Like you."

"Older women?" she protested, looking askance. "I didn't know I'd already crossed the line."

But he was calling her attention down onto the grass again. The two young ladies were talking, leaning close and whispering to each other. They looked as lovely as spring flowers, and careless as children.

"Ah, and there is the other one," he told her. "One is blond and one is dark-haired, you see. A variety to choose from."

She laughed again, though she wasn't sure why. This was beginning to sound a little odd. "What are you talking about?"

He put his head to the side and his gaze trailed down the line of her neck. She could almost feel it, and she couldn't stop her natural reaction to reach up and ward it off with her hand. The ghost of a smile shadowed his eyes.

"I don't much like being managed," he said quietly.

She nodded, tingling from the way he was looking at her. She knew she ought to resist it, that she ought to feel annoyed, maybe get up and speak sharply to him, turn and leave him sitting here on the landing. She ought to. But she wouldn't. "I've noticed," she said.

"Good."

"So I take it, some of the visitors are trying to 'manage' you?"

"Most definitely. It is my Aunt Cordelia's mission

in life to take hold of me and mold me into the sort of man she thinks I should be.''

Cordelia. Yes, she knew who that was. A very important woman in Nabotavian society. She thought she could pick out which one she was just by the way the others were deferring to her down below.

"Your Highness," she said, looking straight at him, "just what is it your aunt wants you to do?''

"She wants me to marry one of those pretty girls, of course.''

Tianna's mouth dropped with outrage. "But you're betrothed.''

He nodded and sighed. "You know, that betrothal business has held me in good stead for years. But lately people are starting to disrespect it. They seem to think I should have fulfilled my obligations by now, and since I haven't, I ought to dump the whole thing.''

"Why…that's outrageous!'' The irony of it all was clear to her, but she brushed it aside. It was one thing for her to want to break the promise made so long ago. It was quite another for outsiders to decide these things for her. And for him.

"You think so?'' He looked thoughtful. "I don't know. It does seem that the days of betrothals have pretty much faded from the scene, don't you think?''

"Not at all,'' she argued stoutly. "These arrangements are made for very specific reasons. And studies show that arranged marriages have a better record of lasting than love relationships do.'' She could hardly believe this was coming from her own mouth. These were the very arguments her own mother had used when she'd chafed under the rules herself.

They hadn't done much to change her own opinion. Why on earth did she think they would work on Garth? And why did she want them to all of a sudden? Looking at him, she realized knowing him was changing her.

"Well, I've loved being betrothed," he went on. "It's kept me safe through many a relationship when I was younger. Whenever some lovely young thing began to speak of commitment, I gently reminded her of the betrothal, and that was that."

No outrage. Not this time. She was getting wise to him. Instead of swallowing his tale whole, she gave him a gimlet eye. "Why are you trying so hard to make me believe you're really a cad?" she asked him.

"What?" He pretended shock at her lack of faith in him. "You don't believe it?"

She favored him with a mysterious smile and turned away.

"Wait. What do I have to do to convince you?"

"I'm not falling for it anymore," she announced. "I think I know you too well." She flashed him a look. "Try as you might, you can't keep me from liking you."

"Liking me?" He sounded surprised, but more than that, he sounded as though her saying that had touched him in some way. "Really?"

Suddenly it seemed too big a confession and she wished she hadn't made it. Confused, she turned to look at Marika, hoping to use fussing with her to hide her consternation, but Marika was sound asleep in her little chair, her arms limp, her breathing soft and even. Tianna's emotions calmed at the sight of her and a smile tilted her lips. Who could resist such a beautiful baby?

She looked up at the prince to see if he was enjoying Marika's charm as well, but found him looking at her, not the baby, with an intensity that startled her.

"Don't."

"Don't what?"

"Look at me like that."

"Can I kiss you instead?"

She swallowed and tried to look unperturbed. "Why me? Why don't you go kiss one of them?" She nodded toward the two young lovelies.

"They are beautiful, aren't they?" He said the words, but his gaze was still on her and it was clear his interest was, too. He even moved his chair closer to where she sat.

"Yes," she said breathlessly. "Beautiful girls. Pick one and kiss *her*."

Slowly, he shook his head. Leaning closer, he touched her cheek with his finger. "I don't want to kiss one of them. I want to kiss you."

Try as she might, her foggy brain couldn't dredge up one good argument against it. "Why?" she asked a bit agitatedly, but as he leaned even closer, she didn't back away.

He shrugged as his arm came around her, pulling

her into the warmth of his body. "You got me," he murmured, burying his face in her silky hair.

"I…I thought we agreed that it would be better not to do things like…like kissing," she said, shivering deliciously.

"I don't remember agreeing to any such thing," he whispered, and then his lips were on hers, making soft love bites, teasing her, enticing her.

She sighed and began to kiss him back. She'd never felt anything as warm and exciting as his touch and she wanted more of it. His kisses were intoxicating, drugging her senses, and she was about to float away on pure sensation.

But his cell phone rang. For a moment, they both ignored it. The second ring came, and he sighed, drawing back. Reaching for it, he flipped it open and said, "Yes?" but his gaze never left her.

She closed her eyes, still drifting in the aftermath of his embrace, feeling foolish but happy anyway.

He listened for a moment. "Alright," he said, just a bit impatiently. "I'll be right down. Tell Cordelia I'm sorry to be so late about it, but I've been delayed by something much more important." One side of his mouth lifted in a semigrin. "Yes, use those exact words. I'll be there in a moment."

Closing the phone he gave her a look of regret and began to pull away from the table.

"We'll be eating at seven in the main dining room. Will you join us?"

Her head came up. Her lips still tingled from touch-

ing his. She wanted to join him in anything, everything—breathing, even. But she had to touch down to
earth again, and reluctantly, she did so.

"Absolutely not," she said, and managed to sound
firm about it. "I'll be eating in the nursery." She felt
she had to remind him. "That's where the nanny belongs, you know."

He gave her a slow grin. "And when did you start
acting like a proper nanny?"

"Do you have any complaints?"

"Not a one. But I have noticed that you tend to act
more like the lady of the manor than you do an employee." He gazed at her quizzically. "Have you noticed that yourself?"

She gave him a look and didn't answer.

"Why don't you come with us?" he coaxed. "It
would be a lot more fun if you were there. You can
sit at my right hand and keep me company."

She laughed just thinking about the looks on the
faces of those women when they realized the nanny
was going to eat with them—sitting in the place of
honor no less! But she really didn't want to risk having
the duchess suddenly jump up, jab a finger in her direction and yell out, "Your Highness, that woman is
an imposter!" That wouldn't go down well and she
still had a job to get done here.

She shook her head. "I'd better stay with Marika,"
she said, and he nodded, giving her one last long look
before departing.

She watched him go, the blood still racing through

her veins in a way she found exhilarating—and very scary. Was Janni right? Had she really fallen for him? And if that was the case, what on earth was she prepared to do about it?

The dinner hour had come and gone and the party had retired to the sitting room. Tianna had finally succeeded in getting Marika to fall asleep and she wanted to do the same as soon as possible. She had only had a couple of hours sleep the night before and she was feeling it. Still, she wanted to get something to read, as she thought chances were good she would be up with Marika again at some point during the night. She was pretty sure she could slip past the sitting room without being seen.

Making her way to the library, all went well. She could hear the laughter and the high female voices, set against the low tone that had to be Garth, and it made her smile. He was quite the king of the hill, alone with all those women.

Then she remembered the pretty young pair and her smile faded. He could make fun all he wanted to, those were very pretty girls. She couldn't deny that she felt a pang of something close to jealousy to think of them spending time with him.

Jealousy! Where had that word come from? She wasn't jealous. She didn't need to be jealous. After all, she was the one who was as good as engaged to the man! Oh, the irony of it all.

"What a tangled web we weave," she muttered as she sped along.

The library was empty, just as she'd thought it would be, and she went immediately to the shelves and began browsing the history section. There was a great selection of volumes on Nabotavian history, and though that hadn't been what she'd thought she would choose when planning her reading, something about the subject drew her attention and she decided it had been too long since she'd read anything on her country of birth. Reaching out, she took three books down and carried them to a large, overstuffed couch where she curled up to leaf through them and make a choice between them.

The first thing she did was to look up the history of the Great Nabotavian Rift of 1860. The rift had cut the country in two, leaving the Roseanovas to rule, but giving her own family a long, thin slice of the country to manage themselves. She had only a sketchy picture of what exactly had happened to force the change, but she quickly found a description.

It seemed her great-great-grandfather—and Garth's— King Marcovo I, was frustrated by the activities of his first son and heir, Marcovo II, who spent his days fox hunting with his dissolute friends, and his nights getting local ladies "with child." One famous minister of the crown was quoted as saying, "At the rate he's going, half the children in the kingdom will soon be claiming the Crown Prince as their daddy."

"Oh my," Tianna said, stifling a giggle. "Garth, you come from the wild side, don't you?"

On the other hand, her own great-grandfather Peter, Marcovo the First's second son—and his favorite—was a serious young man who did his duty and studied voraciously and started the national institute of sciences. Angry that the country had to be handed to his good-for-nothing son, the king decreed that the country be cut along the banks of the Tannabee River, giving Peter a kingdom of his own. The entire area consisted of less than a quarter of the land of Nabotavia, and it was arguably too mountainous and desolate to amount to much. Still, the rest of the government refused to let it leave the actual authority of the Nabotavian kingdom. So Peter was given a sort of paper kingdom, one that was still really a part of Nabotavia, but could pretend to be independent. And, as she well knew, it would exist as a thorn in the side of the Nabotavian royalty from then on. Her marriage to Garth was supposed to heal the rift. But did anyone really care anymore?

She'd just put down one book and picked up the next when she heard voices, and then her place of refuge was invaded by two of the visitors. The couch faced away from the entry side of the room and she sank down into it, out of sight, as she realized one of the women was her mother's friend. Her heart began to skip and she felt downright silly to be hiding. But what could she do? Nothing but wait and hope they left quickly.

"Well, I think it's just senseless the way he's clinging to this betrothal," one of the women was saying. "I know you think a lot of the West Nabotavian royal family and I'm sure they are very nice people, but the point is, they are unimportant people."

Tianna stifled the outrage that rose in her throat. They were talking about her family! Who did this woman think she was? Suddenly she realized she could see both of the newcomers in the large mirror at the end of the room—and that they could see her if they turned in that direction. Her pulse raced, but she was torn between wanting to remain hidden and wanting to rise up and confront this witch.

"Who needs West Nabotavia, after all?" the woman was going on. "It's all mountains. No industry, no society or community to speak of. And these two young things I've brought to meet Garth are the daughters of very rich captains of industry who have a lot of money to throw around. And money is what we're going to need to bring Nabotavia back to glory, believe me."

"Of course, Cordelia," the duchess agreed. "But I don't really understand why you put such stock in Prince Garth. After all, he's not the crown prince."

Cordelia sighed. "I've always had a special warmth for Garth. I often took care of the boys when they were young, you know, and he and I just seemed to have a special rapport." She sighed again. "Besides, he is the only one of the three who bears the mark, you know."

"The mark?"

"The mark of the rose."

"I had no idea."

"Oh yes. And in the traditional position, too. Right over his heart."

Tianna's head lifted and she listened more intently. She'd never heard of this mark of the rose before.

"I'd heard of it years ago, of course, but I thought it was a sort of historical myth. What is it, a birthmark sort of thing?"

"Yes. It looks like a rose just beginning to unfurl its petals. My brother, the late king, God rest his soul... he had it. Our father had it, too. But of the children, only Garth has it. And I can't help but think that the one who has it is specially marked for greatness."

Tianna frowned, trying to remember just what the birthmark she'd seen on Marika had looked like—and where it was placed. It seemed to her it was very much like what Cordelia was describing. How strange. How very, very strange.

"Oh, I see," the duchess was saying agreeably.

"Yes. And that is why I think it is very important who Prince Garth marries. It's a new age. We need fresh blood in the line. These girls both come from dynamic families. Their fathers have done great things. Either one of them would be a wonderful match for Garth. If only I can convince him to void this betrothal."

As though summoned, the prince himself appeared in the doorway. His gaze connected with Tianna's in the mirror. Noting the way she was scrunched down in the couch, he took in the situation at a glance. Quickly, he turned his full smile on the two older women.

"Ladies, dessert is being served," he announced.

"Oh!"

"Please hurry back to the sitting room." He made a sweeping gesture as though ushering them to the door.

"And you?" his aunt asked. "Aren't you going to join us?"

"Of course. I just need a moment, if you don't mind. I have a few things I want to think over."

"Oh, of course." The two ladies started for the door, but Cordelia stopped and turned back. "But tell me, my dear, what do you think of the girls?"

"The girls?" He looked at her blankly for a moment. "Oh, the two young ladies?" He made a move as though to get them started out the door again. "Yes, quite beautiful. And charming."

"Yes," Cordelia said, still resisting the push he was making to get them out of the room. "I'd like you to have a little more time with them before we leave in the morning. You should get to know them better."

"I'll certainly do my best." He put his hand in the middle of her back and literally guided her to the door. "See you in a few minutes," he promised, then closed the door and turned to face Tianna.

"What the hell is going on here?" he demanded.

She rose to face him, her cheeks flushed. "That is

what I'd like to know," she retorted. "So you're going to break your betrothal in order to marry one of those Bobbsey twins? How crass can you get?"

His frown was almost angry. "Who said I was doing any such thing?"

"Cordelia."

He groaned. "My darling Aunt Cordelia has been working her chubby little fingers to the bone trying to get me to do just that," he admitted. "But I told you I didn't like being managed. I have no intention of marrying one of those two empty-headed little flirts."

"Oh." Taking a deep breath, she began to calm down. "That's good."

She started to turn away but he pulled her back, holding her upper arm in his strong hand.

"But why would you care about something like that?" he asked her softly.

She gave him a superior look. "I just wouldn't want to see you throw your integrity away on those… those…" She stopped. What was she doing? The girls were perfectly fine young women for all she knew. If she went on like this, she would sound like a jealous lover. "Oh, never mind," she said, avoiding his gaze and suddenly wishing he would kiss her. "You'd probably better go join your party."

He let go of her arm and she could tell he was drawing away.

"Wait," she said, and this time she was the one who grabbed *his* arm—though she pulled her hand back right away. "Do you know where Janus is?" she asked him. "I haven't seen him all evening."

The prince shrugged. "He must be around somewhere. He laid these clothes out for me to wear."

She looked them over. Sleek and trendy, the suit fit him like a glove, emphasizing his muscular body in a way that would make strong women swoon. "And very handsome they are, too," she admitted.

"Thank you."

He smiled into her eyes and she wanted that kiss again. Could he tell? But if he could, why wasn't he kissing her?

Then she remembered there was something else nagging at her—the mark of the rose that Cordelia had been talking about. She'd better find out anything she could about it while she still had him here.

"Your Highness," she said quickly. "Your aunt said you have the mark of the rose. What did she mean? Is it a tattoo?"

"Actually, it's a sort of birthmark that runs in the family. If you have a really vivid imagination, it looks like a rose. It doesn't pop up on everyone, but I've got it. Marco and my baby sister Kari don't."

"Is it considered special?"

He nodded. "Sort of. It's strongly identified with the House of the Rose. Why?"

The implications were finally coming clear to her. This could be big.

She grabbed his arm more tightly. "I have to show you something. Come with me, quickly."

He put his hand over hers. "What's the matter?"

She shook her head. "Please. Just come with me."

He searched her eyes, frowning, then turned toward where the sounds of silver against china emanated from the sitting room.

"I don't think that would be such a good idea, Tianna. I've promised the others...."

She took a deep breath. Of course, he was right. "Then meet me in the nursery as soon as you can."

"All right." He looked at her curiously. "I'll be there within the hour."

He was as good as his word. Tianna had been pacing the floors waiting for him and when he arrived, she felt relief mixed with apprehension.

Marika was still asleep. Tianna peeled back her little shirt and let him see the mark on her chubby little baby chest, just above her heart. The reddish-brown discoloration was still there, and it most definitely could have been called a rose.

He stared down at it and it seemed to her that for just a moment, he turned to stone. Not saying a word, he very carefully shrugged out of his suit coat, slung it across the back of the chair, then began to unbutton his shirt. She waited, her heart beating in her throat. He slipped out of the shirt and stood silently, his beautiful, muscular body displayed before her. The birthmark, just above his heart, looked very much like the smaller version on Marika's chest.

Tianna was expecting exactly what she saw, but

even so, she gasped when she saw it. It was so perfect. *He* was so perfect. Hesitantly, she reached out and touched the mark with her fingertips, then looked up into his eyes.

Taking her by the shoulders, he pulled her up against him and kissed her, hard on the mouth. The heat from his naked skin burned her, but the kiss only lasted for seconds, and then he put her back where she'd been, slipped back into his shirt, grabbed his jacket, and left the room. The entire time, neither of them had said a word.

Chapter Seven

A baby was crying. Garth tossed and turned in his bed, not sure if he was dreaming or if there really was a baby in distress. Finally he was wide-awake enough to tell the difference. It was for real.

He lay listening. It wasn't so much what he heard as what he felt. Marika was crying. Did that mean *his daughter* was crying? Was she his?

No. She couldn't be. And yet…and yet…

Rolling over, he looked at the clock. It was two in the morning. He lay still for another moment, then began to get up, shaking the sleep from his head, reaching for a sweatshirt and jeans. A few minutes later he was outside the nursery, listening for any evidence of what was going on within.

There it was. Marika's fussy voice, Tianna hushing her. He knocked softly on the door, then let himself in.

"Oh." Tianna looked dead tired as she gazed at him from the middle of the room. She was holding Marika, whose face was red and blotchy and wet with tears. She'd obviously been pacing the floor with the baby for a very long time. "Did we wake you up? I'm sorry."

"No problem," he said. "Here. Let me take her."

He reached for her and Marika's little arms shot out, ready to be taken. She babbled something unintelligible and actually seemed to be smiling through her tears. Tianna released her and Garth took the weight of her in his arms. Life, warm and sweet and magic. He seemed to know just how to hold her now. She fit in his arms as though she'd been born to be there. Marika. Was she…?

He looked up at Tianna. Her eyes were shadowed by dark smudges, but she was still as beautiful as ever in the dim lamplight, standing there in her lacy nightgown, covered by a soft blue robe.

"Get in bed," he told her. "You're dying for some sleep. I'll take care of Marika."

She stared at him. "What?" she said, as though she didn't understand.

"I can do it," he reassured her. "I can walk around patting her back as well as you can. And if she falls asleep, I'll put her down in her crib and go back to my room."

"But…but what if…?"

"I'll wake you up." He gestured toward the bed with a nod. "Go on. Get in there."

A slow smile began to grow, first in her eyes, then to include her wide mouth. "When did you become the nurturing one?" she asked, but she started toward the bed, slipping out of her robe and sliding beneath the covers. She sighed, but she still looked tense. "I don't know if this will do any good," she told him. "I'm so wound up, I can't relax."

He'd started to pace the room with the baby to his shoulder. The space was long enough to allow ten steps before he had to turn and go back. Marika gave a shuddering sigh and put her head down, but he could feel that she was far from sleep. Just as Tianna was.

"Why don't you talk for a while?" he suggested. "That might help you let go."

She considered, nestling into the pillow. "What shall I talk about?"

"I don't know." He dropped a kiss on Marika's head and glanced at where Tianna lay, her beautiful hair spread out around her head. "Talk about your favorite movie. Or the latest good book you read. Or— how about this—why did you form such a deep attachment to this baby so quickly? I have a feeling there must be a background to it."

"Oh." She snuggled into the fluffy pillow. "All right." Drawing in a deep breath, she began. "I was five years old during the escape. In the confusion, I was separated from my family. My old nursemaid took me across Europe, racing to the sea where I was supposed to meet up with my family. But something happened and I was placed aboard the wrong boat, and from then on, strangers took care of me. They were kind enough, but I remember being so alone and so cold and so very frightened. I wanted my mother and they couldn't tell me where she was. I think these people didn't really know for sure who I was. I was shuttled from one Nabotavian immigrant community to another. It was almost six months before my parents managed to make it to the States and another few months of looking before they found me.'' Her voice grew softer. ''By then, they said I wouldn't talk. And even after I was reunited with my family, it was months before I would say anything.''

''Poor Tianna.'' He thought of her as a child and smiled. ''I'm sorry you had to go through that.''

She sighed. ''That, or something like it, happened to all of us, didn't it? A lot had it worse than I did. You…well, you lost your parents for good. And that is so much worse. Still, my experience stayed with me in ways I am still only starting to understand. And when I saw that helpless little baby lying there, all alone, her mother gone…'' Her voice broke and she paused for a moment, regaining her composure. ''Well, I just had to make sure she wasn't hurt in any way, if I could help it.''

The baby against his shoulder was still moving, but he risked sitting in the rocking chair and she seemed to respond favorably while he gently rocked her. He understood only too well what Tianna had been telling him. His experience in the escape was still with him as well. He imagined it would probably color the rest of his life.

"How about you?" she said sleepily. "You said Janus got you out. What happened when you got to the States?"

"We were shuttled about, just like you were, at first. Though we were staying with people we knew, so it wasn't quite as bad. Marco was the oldest, and the crown prince, so he was expected to be almost an adult. They were always including him in meetings and things that were way above his years and experience. And Kari was just a baby." Funny how Cook bringing up the memory of him carrying Kari around had opened up a whole chapter of his life he'd pretty much forgotten about. "So I took care of her. We used to hide together, so they wouldn't make us eat oatmeal." He smiled as more memories flooded him. "Finally our father's half brother and his wife, the duke and duchess of Gavini, took Kari to live in Beverly Hills, and our uncle Kenneth brought Marco and me here to Arizona to live in his castle."

"That's right," she said, yawning. "I'd forgotten about him. Where is he now?"

"He went to Nabotavia last year with me when we were working with the underground, and he stayed on."

She didn't say anything in response and he looked over at the bed. Her breathing was even. She was finally asleep. He stayed where he was, watching her sleep, watching her breathe. What was it about this woman that set her apart from all the rest? In a short time she'd become very important to him—indispensable. He didn't like to feel that anyone was that vital to his own well-being. He was always the one in control, the one who could let go and not look back. But things were changing.

Maybe it had something to do with the return to Nabotavia. Maybe it had something to do with his time in the life cycle. He didn't know for sure, but he knew he didn't want to lose her. What, exactly, was he willing to do to make sure that didn't happen? That was the question. And for that, he didn't have an answer yet.

Marika fell asleep against him, but he didn't rise and put her in her crib. He didn't want to risk waking her. Instead, he sank down into the chair with the adorable baby in his arms and fell asleep as well.

Tianna woke in the first light and saw Garth in the chair with Marika. Laughing softly, she slipped out of bed, dropped a soft kiss on the prince's cheek before she took the baby from his arms and carried her to bed. When she turned, she found that he'd already come to his feet and looked ready to leave.

"Everything okay?" he asked, wincing in the light.

She nodded, looking at him with love in her eyes. He smiled and touched her chin with his forefinger.

"What do you think?" he asked her softly. "Do you think she's mine?"

Her eyes clouded and she shook her head. "That's up to you," she told him.

He nodded. "I still can't see how it could be possible. But there are so many signs pointing that way."

Tianna took a deep breath and said something she knew she probably shouldn't. "Could...could she be Marco's?"

His eyes widened and he choked. "Don't make me laugh. Marco is as straight-arrow as they come. He's not like me."

"There's nothing wrong with you," she said defensively.

He looked at her oddly, wondering why she felt that way. "In a strange way I always felt I had to protect Marco," he admitted slowly. "I always tried to keep the real world away from him. He was always so good."

"You're good, too."

"No. Not like Marco." He looked into her eyes for a long moment, feeling a sweeping wave of affection for her, along with the usual sensual interest. She was the one who was good. And goodness like that was a rare trait. Knowing her almost made him believe that a world without lies and treachery was possible. Almost. But not quite.

His mouth touched hers. Her lips parted and his tongue played with hers. She felt so good against him. He could close his eyes and still see her, every detail. He'd memorized her, her smell, the feel of her skin, her voice. And soon, he would know her body as well.

But he was the one who was dead tired now. He felt like death. Drawing back, he told her, "I'm going to go get some sleep. Wake me if anything momentous happens."

"I will."

Watching him go, an apprehensive excitement crept over her. There was no use denying it any longer. She was falling for him all right. Falling pretty hard.

But you've only known him for two days!

True. And untrue. In some ways, she'd known him all her life.

"And after all," she whispered to herself. "We're engaged."

For some time that morning, she could hear the sounds of the cousins packing up and marching down to the limousines. Finally it was quiet and she assumed they had gone. A few hours later, after breakfast and playtime for Marika, a knock came on the nursery door.

"Miss," Bridget called. "Come quickly. Prince Marco wants to see you."

"What?" Tianna opened the door and stared at Bridget in surprise. "He's here?"

"Yes, Miss. He's in the study and he said, please come right away, and bring the baby."

"Of course."

She said the words automatically, but she swallowed hard and had to steady herself before getting together the wits to do as she'd been asked. The crown prince was, after all, the putative king of Nabotavia, and as such, he was the top authority figure in her culture. Prince Garth must have told him about the baby and the unusual bits of evidence that she might be connected in some way to the royal family. And of course, he would want that confirmed or proven false right away.

"Come on, Marika," she said at last. "We're going to see the king."

He was sitting behind the wide desk in the study, but rose when she entered the room, and came toward her, nodding politely but obviously interested in Marika most of all.

"So this is the mysterious baby," he said. "What a beautiful child."

Tianna found herself tongue-tied, which was rare for her. The man had the presence one would expect of royalty, and was just as handsome as his brother, though in a very different way. He had a lean, wiry-looking body, strong without being ostentatiously muscular, reserved rather than friendly. Handsome in a rugged sense, his face had a rather gaunt look, as though he'd been through too much too early in his relatively short existence. She thought she could see evidence of his haunting agony from losing his young wife reflected in his dark eyes. All in all, she was impressed.

"May I see the mark on her chest?"

"Oh. Of course." She pulled back the shirt to show him.

He nodded and she put it back again. Suddenly she found him looking straight into her eyes, as though he were ordering her to reveal the truth, and she gulped, ready to bare her soul if need be.

"There's been some talk that since you arrived at the same time the baby did, and you have been such a staunch advocate for her, there must be some connection which precedes your arrival."

"No, Your Royal Highness," she managed to stutter out. "I'm afraid that is not correct. I can understand how that misapprehension could come about, but it has no approximation to reality."

He stared at her for a long moment, then smiled coolly. "I'll accept your word on that. Still, it is strange, isn't it? The name, the cloth, the birthmark, all implying a direct connection to the royal family."

"Yes."

"Well, there is obviously only one thing to be done."

"What is that?"

"A DNA test, of course. I've brought a professional with me. He'll do a swab from inside the baby's cheek and compare it to the family DNA. It should take a few days to get the results, and then we will know for sure."

"Oh. Of course."

He bowed and turned back toward the desk, and she realized she'd been dismissed. Holding Marika to her chest, she started back to the nursery, then thought better of it and made a detour. She found Bridget in the library and asked her to take the baby up to the nursery and wait. That done, she took a deep breath and started for the second floor. She knew which room was Garth's and she went to his door, knocking softly.

He opened the door as though he'd been expecting her, and the next thing she knew, she was wrapped in his arms and being kissed like there was no tomorrow—delightfully kissed, hungrily kissed, deliciously kissed. But still, she pulled away, laughing.

"Hey," she said, gazing at him lovingly. "I didn't come here for this. We've got to talk."

He put his head to the side, considering her. "Okay," he allowed. "We'll talk. Then we'll kiss. And then…"

She laughed softly, pressing her palm to his cheek and enjoying the light in his eyes. "Now be good," she told him. "I've just met your brother."

"Marco?" He turned his face and put a kiss right in the center of her palm. "Good old Marco. I told him all about Marika. I suppose he's ordered DNA testing, hasn't he?"

"Yes." She turned away and looked at his room. Larger than the average living room in a normal house, it was lined with bookcases, most of which were taken up with a beautiful stereo system. A huge bed filled one side of the room, and French doors opened onto a terrace balcony.

Turning, she browsed along the bookcases and came upon a very expensive camera.

"Nice piece of equipment," she said, picking it up

and getting a feel for it, admiring the optical zoom lens.

"I haven't used it much. Go ahead and try it out if you like. Why don't you take some portraits of Marika?"

She set the camera down and turned back toward him. "I don't really have any experience with baby pictures."

He shrugged. "What's special about baby pictures?"

"Nothing. It's just that my field is architecture. You know, skyscrapers against the sky, interesting entryways, angles and crannies. That sort of thing."

"You're going to be like a kid in a candy store if you go back to Nabotavia."

Her eyebrows rose. "How so?"

"The revolution was over in hours and this recent fight to throw off the usurpers only lasted a few days. Not many buildings were damaged. You'll be amazed. It looks like a little piece of nineteenth-century Europe in Kalavia, the capital. And since Nabotavia has been cut off from the rest of the world for the last twenty years, the beauty of our cities is relatively unknown."

"Really? That is interesting." And it was. The idea of being one of the first to document the architectural scenes in the newly liberated country intrigued her for a moment. She was beginning to realize how little she really knew about the old country.

But she did know one thing—she was in love with its prince. Looking at him, a wave of pure affection surged in her chest, making her gasp with its intensity. And the beautiful thing was, he seemed to feel something for her, if evidence was to be believed. Still, one thing stood between finding out how real this feeling was. She was living a lie. How was she going to tell him who she really was? And when?

He came toward her and she knew he was getting impatient. Coming close, he took her face in his hands and looked down into her eyes.

"I've been trying to figure out what I like about you," he said softly as he studied her face.

"Difficult to pin down, isn't it?" she teased. "There's just so much to choose from."

"Exactly." He smiled. "You're beautiful, of course. You're good. You're loving. You care about people." He dropped a kiss on her soft lips and sighed happily. "But I think the thing that gives you that special edge is your basic bedrock honesty."

Her heart jumped, but this time with dismay. "No," she said softly, shaking her head with warning. "No, it's not that."

"Why not?"

"Don't you know? I'm lying to you all the time."

He laughed, not taking her seriously. "And that's another thing," he said. "You do have a sense of humor." He kissed her again. "You couldn't lie if you tried."

"Oh Garth," she wailed, but he didn't let her get any more words out.

His mouth covered hers, hot and urgent, and she

tried at first to push him away, to catch her breath so she could make some attempt at telling him the truth. It was time. It was way past time. She should have told him before…should never have let him think she was not who she really was…should have known her playacting would get her in trouble.

But all those fears faded as his kisses did the work of changing the subject for her. Very quickly, she forgot what she'd been worrying about, forgot that there was ever anything to worry about. Life seemed too good for worrying. In the arms of this strong, wonderful man, she felt safe and adored in a way she never had before. Sinking into the sensual fog he created around them, she needed his touch, craved the taste of his mouth, delighted in the scent of his skin, loved the sound of his husky voice uttering sweet nonsense in her ear. Every kiss made her hungry for more, and the sense of need began to build in her very quickly.

When his hand slid under her sweater and cupped her breast, she sighed with pleasure, and suddenly she wanted to feel his muscular chest under her hands, wanted to press herself to him with nothing in between them, wanted to feel her breasts rub against his naked skin. The shock of recognition flashed through her. She wanted to make love.

''Oh!'' She drew back, staring at him, her eyes very wide. ''Wait a minute,'' she said breathlessly. ''Hold it. What the heck is going on here?''

He laughed down at her, keeping her in the circle

of his arms. "I don't know, Tianna. What do you think is going on?"

"We're going to end up in bed," she warned, her eyes flashing. "I feel like I was just on the edge of a cliff and about to leap over. One more minute of that and…" Her voice trailed off and she shook her head in wonder.

Chuckling, he kissed her lips, then nuzzled her ear. "You're damn right we're going to end up in bed," he told her softly, his breath hot on her neck. "Not today. But soon."

"You think so?" she asked him, melting against his body again.

"I know it, Tianna." He held her face in his hands and his eyes lost all trace of amusement. "It's meant to be," he said, very seriously.

She searched his eyes, then nodded, slowly. "It's meant to be," she repeated.

But what would happen once he found out how true that was?

Chapter Eight

Tianna knew it was time to tell Garth the truth about her identity. She wasn't sure how he was going to react once he found out. He would be annoyed, of course. Anyone would be. But maybe he would be as amused as she was with the fact that a match that had been set up when they were children was turning out to be more or less made in heaven after all.

Would they end up getting married? She had no idea. But she knew it was past time to let him in on the facts, so he could consider that, too.

She finally worked up the courage to spill the beans and she started toward the library where she thought he might be, to get it done. But the library was empty and when she turned toward the kitchen, she found him hurrying toward her along the hallway.

His face was set and his eyes were stormy. Taking

hold of her arms, he held her before him. "Marco and I are going to Los Angeles right away. There's a helicopter landing on the grounds to get us to the airport more quickly."

As he spoke, she thought she could hear the sound of the rotor blades. "Garth, what's happened?"

He took a deep breath. "My sister Kari has been kidnapped. I don't have time to give you all the details. We're going right now. But Tianna—" he pulled her in closer, his gaze holding hers "—promise me you and Marika will be here when I get back."

She looked up at him, surprised that he would even have any fears along those lines. "Of course we'll be here. I promise."

His gaze darkened and he kissed her firmly on the mouth. "You're such a mystery to me, Tianna. You came out of nowhere and changed everything. I suddenly had this crazy feeling that you might disappear just as mysteriously."

For no reason she could put her finger on, tears filled her eyes. "I'll be here," she whispered to him. "I'll wait for you."

He kissed her again and turned to go without another backward glance. She ran to the windows on the landing, watching as he and Marco hurried to the helicopter. And then she gasped, because Janus was coming quickly behind them. Janus, who had been avoiding her like the plague—he was going too.

"Janus!" she said aloud, knowing he couldn't hear

her. "What's the deal? I want to know what you've found out!"

Of course, there was no answer. He certainly wasn't going to do much searching in Los Angeles. She fumed, but there wasn't anything she could do about it now. She stayed where she was, watching the helicopter lift off, hover for a moment, then whisk away in the direction of the airport. She hoped they would get to Los Angeles in time, prayed that Kari would be unhurt. But she couldn't stop wondering about Janus and his strange behavior.

An hour later, with Marika asleep, she had made her decision. If Janus wasn't working on finding Marika's mother, she was going to have to do it herself. The problem was, where to start?

Had Janus checked the doctors in town? Had he contacted the hospitals and investigated births from the period when Marika would have been born? She just didn't know. So what should she do?

"Why not start at the beginning?" she muttered to herself. Hadn't Cook said that when foundlings were sent to the orphanage, they conducted their own investigations? Why not call there and get some recommendations on what to do? Maybe they could give her the name of a professional investigator who specialized in these matters.

Looking the number up, she dialed it and asked to speak to the head of the orphanage. Unfortunately the woman was out and not due back until late that evening, and the receptionist who took the call didn't sound competent to give out the time of day, much less investigating advice, so Tianna would have to wait.

There wasn't much to do other than take care of Marika and worry about Princess Kari. She called her sister to let her know about what was going on, and Janni was suitably anxious about Princess Karina's fate. But she also had some rather disturbing news of her own.

"Father wants to talk to you," she told Tianna. "I told him you were out sightseeing and couldn't be contacted, but he's not going to be satisfied with that for long."

"Why does he want to talk to me?"

"That's just it. I don't know. He's had a couple of long phone calls and he and Mother have been conferring in whispered meetings all over the house. Of course, I'm not invited to share in the discussions, seeing as how I'm the black sheep of the family. Or would that be 'sheepess'? 'Sheepette'? 'Black ewe'?"

"Janni!"

"Sorry. At any rate, I'm out of the loop. But after all this conferring, he told me he had to talk to you. I think you'd better call him."

Tianna sighed. She really wasn't up to it just now. "Tomorrow," she promised, and rang off.

Then she went back down to be with the others and worry. Cook and Milla and all the rest of the staff spent most of the day wringing their hands and asking if anyone had heard anything. The princess was very popular with them all.

"Oh, if this gets into the papers," Cook fretted. "You know we do hate that."

Tianna nodded. She understood the feeling. "It's been my impression that the Nabotavian royal family has been rather good at staying out of the tabloids," she noted.

"Exactly. The house of Roseanova is determined to avoid ending up as fodder for the scandal rags like most of the European families. It's all so demeaning."

"Well, a kidnapping is pretty hard to keep away from the press," Tianna said. "We'll just have to wait and see."

Finally the call came. "She's been rescued!" cried Cook, who answered the phone. "She's just fine."

Cheers erupted all through the house and out in the yard where the chauffeurs and gardeners were gathered as well.

"Prince Garth would like to speak to you," Cook said, handing the receiver to Tianna. "Now the rest of you get back to work."

Tianna felt her cheeks flush as everyone in the kitchen turned to look at her.

"Hello?" she said.

"Hello." Prince Garth's rich voice sent a thrill cartwheeling through her soul. "I just wanted you to know Kari is fine."

Quickly, he outlined what had happened, how Kari had been kidnapped by a group allied with the defeated rebels in Nabotavia, how a security guard named Jack Santini had stormed up the ramp of the airplane the kidnappers were using for their getaway and grabbed the princess right out of their clutches.

"And now, believe it or not, it looks like the two of them will be getting married."

"The princess and the security guard?"

"That's Sir Security Guard to you," Garth told her, chuckling. "Marco has knighted him. At any rate, we'll be coming home in the morning. I'll tell you all the rest when we get there."

"Good."

"I miss you."

She glanced around the kitchen. Everyone was finally hard at work and didn't seem to be paying any attention any longer. "I miss you, too," she whispered into the receiver. "And so does Marika."

It was only after she hung up that she realized she hadn't thought to ask about Janus. Well, there would be time to deal with that the next day, once they were all back and she could confront Janus on her own—something she was itching to do. It made her crazy to think he might have actively hindered their search for the mother. Had he? She had no proof. But she was beginning to wonder.

And by the middle of the next day, she would wonder even more. She got up early and changed and fed Marika, then gave her to Bridget for safekeeping while she went to call the orphanage.

"My name is Tianna Rose," she said once she had the manager on the phone. "I'm staying at the castle. I understand you have an outbreak of chicken pox there at the orphanage and…"

"What?"

"Chicken pox." Tianna blinked. She hadn't meant to get bogged down at this point. She was only launching here. "I had heard you couldn't accept any new orphans until you had handled your chicken pox situation."

"I don't know where you got that information. We have no chicken pox problem. Haven't had one in years."

Tianna paused. This was certainly odd. "Are you telling me you could accept new babies right now?"

"Of course. We've had no restrictions at all this year."

"I see," she said slowly. "Well…thank you very much."

She didn't pursue her original intentions. This little bombshell needed to be fully explored first. Sitting very still, she tried to remember just what had happened that first day. Cook had sent Milla to call the orphanage, and Milla had come back saying they had chicken pox and couldn't accept any new babies for the time being. She remembered that distinctly. What exactly was going on here?

Rising, she marched very deliberately down to the kitchen and strode through the double doors.

"Milla," she said, trying to remain calm. "May I have a word with you?"

"Of course, Miss." The young maid came bouncing over to where Tianna stood waiting for her. "What can I do for you?"

Tianna did not answer her smile. "You can tell me why you told us that the orphanage had chicken pox."

Milla looked startled. "Oh."

"The orphanage claims there has been no such thing. So why did you say so?"

"Oh, but that is what Mr. Janus told me. I didn't call them. I went to call them, but Mr. Janus, he said he would do it, and he came back very quickly and told me about the chicken pox."

Tianna felt thunderstruck. "Janus told you that?"

"Yes, Miss." She nodded her head energetically. "I have to take Mr. Janus's lead, you know. If he says, 'I'll do it,' I have to let him."

"Of course you do." Tianna's shoulders sagged but her mind was racing. Janus, once again. What was his angle? She had to think this over. They wouldn't be back until late in the afternoon. That gave her a lot of time. Probably too much time.

The day dragged. She thought about calling her father, but she didn't want to. If she talked to him, she would have to lie. And despite all this craziness she'd been living here at the castle, she hated lying.

Of course, she told herself quickly, she hadn't really lied as yet. She'd just let people believe things that weren't quite the truth. *Which is as good as a lie,*

Tianna, she heard her mother's voice saying. And she knew the voice was right.

Yes, it was way past time to begin telling the truth. She had to tell the prince who she really was, and she had to do it right away. Suddenly, she was impatient to tell him. She couldn't imagine how she could have left it so long. She had to clear the slate.

Finally she heard the car coming up the drive. She was tempted to run down to greet them, but she knew that wouldn't be wise. Better to be patient. Dressing Marika in a pretty pink outfit she found in the closet, she waited, and when she couldn't stand it any longer, she went to the kitchen.

"Have you heard?" Bridget cried as she passed her in the kitchen doorway. "There's going to be a wedding!"

"A wedding?"

She turned, looking after her. *Whose?*

"As if we didn't have enough on our plate," Cook was fussing. "And now a wedding. And in seven days. How am I supposed to prepare for a wedding in seven days? Can't be done!"

"What's this wedding?" Tianna asked.

"Why, Princess Karina and her fiancé, haven't you heard? They are coming here in just a few days and we're supposed to put on a wedding. It's impossible."

Things were already in a frenzy, so Tianna turned and left the kitchen. And practically ran into Prince Garth in the hallway.

"Ah, there you are," he said. He reached for Marika, but his gaze was taking in everything he could get of Tianna.

"Hello," she said, glowing. She wanted a kiss very badly, but she knew it would be too risky here in the hallway. "I hear there's a wedding in the works."

"Yes. A very small wedding. Just the immediate family, really." He grimaced. "We want to get it done before the tabloids get wind of it. They were already crawling all over the house in Beverly Hills, wanting stories about the kidnapping." Giving Marika a big kiss on her round cheek, he handed her back. "You're looking very beautiful this afternoon," he told Tianna softly.

She grinned at him happily. "You don't look so bad yourself," she told him. Then she remembered some more sobering issues. "Where is Janus? I need to talk to him."

"Janus stayed behind to help Kari pack up and move her things here to Arizona."

"Oh no." Quickly she explained why she was afraid that Janus had been hindering rather than helping in the search for Marika's mother.

The prince was worried, but skeptical as he thought over what she told him. "Tianna, that doesn't make any sense. Why would he want the baby kept here rather than at the orphanage? Why would he care?"

"That's just it. Why does he care? Why did he do the things he seems to have done?"

The prince frowned, shaking his head. Finally, he looked into her eyes and said earnestly, "Listen. Janus was like a substitute father to me when I was growing up. He's still one of the closest human beings in my life. You're going to have to give me more evidence than this before I will start suspecting him of doing anything underhanded.''

She knew this was hard for him to take. It was hard for her as well and she didn't have the same emotional attachment to the man. "I don't want to condemn him any more than you do," she protested. "I just want some answers.''

He nodded thoughtfully. "We'll talk to him when he gets back." He had the restless look of a man with things to do and he started to turn away.

"One more thing," she said, stopping him with a hand on his arm. "I need some time to talk to you tonight.''

"Talk?'' He brushed her face fleetingly with the palm of his hand, his eyes darkening as he looked into hers. "Let's make out instead.''

"I'm serious. I have to tell you something.''

"About Marika?''

"No. About me.''

He looked puzzled. "Oh. Why can't you tell me now?''

She took a deep breath. "I need a little time. And privacy.''

"All right. But it's going to have to be rather late. We have a visitor coming soon. I'll be tied up with him until dinnertime, at least. So after dinner?''

She nodded.

"Okay."

"I'm glad you're back," she whispered as he turned to go.

He looked back and smiled. "Me, too."

An hour later, she knew the mysterious visitor had arrived and she wondered idly who it might be. She'd asked, but everyone was being a little cagey, which only piqued her interest. As the afternoon stretched toward evening, she grew restless. Marika was asleep and she had nothing much to do, so she decided to take a stroll past the study to see if she could figure out what was going on.

To her surprise, voices were being raised behind the study door. She paused, listening. There seemed to be a pretty strenuous argument in progress. And something about one of the voices sounded very familiar, but for the moment, she couldn't place it. Then she thought she heard her own name spoken. This had gone beyond curiosity. If she was being discussed, she was darn well going to find out why.

Throwing open the door, she marched into the study. And then wished she could march right out again. There in the room were Crown Prince Marco, Prince Garth, a man who looked very much like a lawyer, and last but not least, her very own father. Oops.

He bolted from his chair, staring at her. "Katianna!" he cried, his usually handsome face red, though probably from some previous shouting. "What are you doing here?"

"Uh...visiting?" She tried to smile. "Hello, Father."

Garth rose, too, staring at first Tianna, then her parent. "What does this mean?" he said, bewildered.

But Trandem Roseanova-Krimorova, king of West Nabotavia, wasn't paying attention to him. He was too busy being furious with his daughter.

"So you are conspiring behind my back!" he roared at her. "Katianna, what have you done to make this man no longer want to honor his betrothal to you?"

"What?" She turned to look at Garth. "You're breaking our betrothal?"

The prince shook his head. "Who the hell *are* you?" he demanded, his eyes burning.

She winced at his tone. "I'm Katianna, princess of West Nabotavia. The one you are betrothed to. That's what I was going to tell you later on tonight."

He shook his head, looking as though he could hardly believe it, or his eyes. "You tricked me."

"No!"

A shadow of some strange form of agony filled his eyes. "What the hell...?"

But their own conversation was getting drowned out by her father's rant.

"Father, wait," she said, shaking her head at him. "Stop shouting and tell me why you're here."

"Why am I here? To try to stop our family from being swindled, that's why I'm here. I received a communication from this shyster of a lawyer telling me the prince wanted to break off the betrothal so I rushed down here to have a face-to-face meeting with him. And now I find that you are somehow involved in this travesty. Aren't you?''

"Well, sort of…''

"I have told you before. The betrothal stands. I will not rescind it. This was a bargain made years ago between me and King Marcovo, to heal the wounds of four generations of Nabotavian royalty. Our country needs this to bind it together. The selfish concerns of you two are of no interest to me. You will do this for the good of your country.'' Seemingly satisfied that he'd made his point with her, he turned back to the others. "The arrogant Roseanova family once again thinks it can lord it over the rest of us and dictate what we can and cannot do. Well, I won't stand for it.'' He frowned fiercely. "I haven't been the best, most attentive king in the world, but at least I will have the reunited nation of Nabotavia as my legacy.'' He pointed his finger at Prince Garth. "You are going to marry my daughter. It's time we discussed a date.''

Complete silence met his demand. No one seemed to know what to say. Her father went back to grumbling, but Tianna could tell the brunt of his anger was spent and she hardly listened. Her attention was all on Garth. She still needed to explain to him, but what she saw in his face didn't give her a lot of hope that he would understand.

* * *

It was an hour later before things calmed down and they had a chance to talk. They met in the library. She walked in hesitantly and noticed right away that his eyes didn't have their usual warmth. If only she could think of some way to make him understand how it had all come about almost without her knowing it.

"Well, I feel like a proper fool," he said, looking down at her, his face hard and unreadable.

She shook her head helplessly. There was really no reason for him to feel that way, but she didn't know how to make him stop. "I'm so sorry."

"What was the point of lying to me?"

"Well, I didn't…technically I didn't really lie, I just…"

His gaze was cold. "You thought you would come play a joke on us?"

"Oh, no!"

"You came to check us out, see if you thought you could stomach the prospect of marrying me?"

"Garth, that wasn't it at all…"

"Then what? Why did you come here?"

She took a deep breath and then looked beseechingly into his eyes, willing him to understand. "I came to talk you into breaking the betrothal."

He stared at her for a moment, then gave a mirthless laugh. "I've got a headache."

"No, listen. I told you I wanted to take a job in Chicago. I came to see if you were as disenchanted with the idea of marriage as I was, and if so, maybe we could work on doing something about it."

"If that was your object, you took a long enough time getting around to it." He shook his head. "Sorry, Princess. I don't buy it. I don't know why you did this, but I really wish you hadn't. It's going to take me some time to digest it all." He walked toward the door, then looked back. "You were the one person I thought I could count on," he said softly, his eyes haunted. And then he was gone.

She stayed behind, feeling numb. She'd known he would be upset, but she hadn't expected this. For the first time, she faced the possibility that he might not get over it. That whatever had been sparked between them might be dead, forever. And that was a fate she dreaded.

Chapter Nine

The story of Tianna's true identity spread through the castle faster than a summer cold and Tianna had to endure her share of stares and whispers. Cook tried to get her to move into a more elegant bedroom, but she refused. She also refused a direct order from her father to accompany him back to Seattle. She was Marika's nanny for the duration. Once the baby's fate was settled, she would leave. Until then, she was staying. Her first and most important objective had been protecting the child, and she would see her task through to completion.

The next couple of days passed quickly, which was lucky, because she was in misery most of the time. The staff obviously felt awkward around her, not sure how to treat her now. Prince Marco seemed cool and removed. And Prince Garth seemed to see right through her most of the time. He was hurt and angry and she didn't blame him. But she thought he should let her give her side to it all. And so far, he hadn't wanted to talk.

Meanwhile, she used every spare moment to look for Marika's mother. The orphanage referred her to a good investigator, but he was out of town for the week, so she was on her own. She called every hospital, every woman's shelter, every doctor's office in the area, but no one could remember a single mother giving birth to a little girl in the time frame she gave them. And no one mentioned that anyone else had recently called, asking the same question. So much for Janus and his search.

But soon she was caught up in the preparations for the wedding, too, making place cards for the banquet, designing flower arrangements for the tables and the chapel, calling around for the best prices on supplies.

"A small wedding," Garth had said. His idea of small wasn't hers. Over two hundred people were coming. No wonder Cook was nearly hysterical.

"This will be the end of me," she moaned over and over as she hurried from one task to the next.

The saying made Tianna wince. Somehow it seemed a bad omen, spelling doom all around. She didn't want to think that way, not now, while everyone was so excited about the wedding. But she just couldn't shake the feeling that everything was going wrong.

Princess Karina arrived on the fourth day. She recognized Tianna right away, and they hugged and she exclaimed over the baby. She didn't seem to find it strange that Tianna was there, or that she was acting as nanny. Perhaps it was because her mind was fixated on Jack Santini and his many virtues, and that was all she seemed to want to talk about.

Unfortunately, Janus wasn't with her.

"He's wrapping up some details in Los Angeles and will be coming soon," Princess Kari told her airily.

That was disappointing. But Tianna and Kari hit it off right from the first, and soon Tianna found herself deeply enmeshed in the princess's personal preparations for the ceremony, including helping with the dress, picking out a veil, choosing a cake style.

"Think of this as a dress rehearsal for your own wedding," she told Tianna breezily. "I hope I'll get to help you out when you and Garth get married."

Tianna murmured something polite, but she wasn't sure there would ever be a wedding. And did she even want one? What had happened to wanting the job in Chicago? Why had she let go of that dream so easily?

"Because you've fallen in love," came the answer. So maybe she should change the question.

She had a talk or two with Garth, but they were brief and always ended in hostility. She tried to explain to him why finding the baby had thrown everything off balance and ended up leaving her pretending to be something she wasn't. She reminded him of her own background.

"I remember that fear I felt as a child, and when I

look at Marika, I can't stand to think of her going through anything like that and growing up with that fear always in her heart. I had good parents. They helped me get over it. But what will she have? I want her to grow up feeling loved and secure, and always welcome in this world, the way every child should. And that is why I didn't announce who I am. I thought I could protect her interests better…''

"You still could have told me the truth," he said stubbornly. "I believed in you."

That was what hurt the most—having disappointed him. Every time he looked at her with that hollowness in his eyes, it cut like a knife.

"Why were you trying to break our betrothal?" she asked him at one point.

He looked at her coldly. "Because I was pretty sure I was falling in love with you," he said. "Or with Tianna Rose, loyal nanny, at any rate. So I wanted to be free."

She heard his words and thrilled to them, but then hopes were dashed. He was describing how things had been, not how they were. She shook her head. "That's real irony, isn't it? You were casting me off in order to keep me."

He didn't seem to find it amusing at all.

"Tell me this," she said, steeling herself for the answer. "Are you still determined to break free of the betrothal?"

His dark eyes clouded. "Are you?" he asked in return.

She stared back at him, and neither of them said another word.

Princess Karina had an epiphany.

"Be my maid of honor!" she cried impulsively. "My friend Donna will be here to be a bridesmaid, but I'd like you to stand beside me."

"I'd love to," Tianna told her, so it was settled. And now there was another dress to think about.

Kari was completely wrapped up in preparations for her wedding and floating on a cloud of pure joy, but even from that vantage point, she could see that something was wrong between her brother and their visitor. She asked Tianna about it and her new close friend filled her in on all the details—hesitantly at first, and then in an emotional rush that gave full evidence to how much she cared for Prince Garth.

And Kari went right to her brother, sure she could fix this in no time at all.

"What is your problem?" she demanded once she'd set up her subject. "Forgive her for that small masquerade and get on with life."

The prince looked at his beautiful little sister moodily. They were both in the rose garden, and the day was gorgeous, all blue sky and golden sunshine. "Don't worry about me, Kari. I'm doing fine."

"If this is 'fine,' I'd hate to see 'poorly.'" She shook her head. "And even if you can stand it, you're hurting Tianna. She loves you, you know."

His smile was bittersweet. "And you, in your innocence, think that love is all that matters."

Her eyes flashed. "I'm not a ninny. I know other things figure in. Some of them very strongly." She put a hand on his arm. "But love is like water. It is necessary to sustain life. And once you find it, you'd better drink deeply, oh brother of mine. Because you might not find a reservoir like this again."

He loved her for her concern. And he loved Tianna. There was no getting around that. But he couldn't trust Tianna. Could he build a life with her this way? When every time he looked at her, he remembered her deception, and with that memory came others, of the days of the Escape, when lies told to him had caused the deaths of his beloved mother and father?

He was overreacting and he knew it. But emotions were hard to control. Maybe, with time, these thoughts would fade. But did they have that much time?

Even though Garth didn't seem to want to be alone with Tianna, he did take Marika for a little while each day. She assumed that meant he was beginning to accept that Marika was his child and she loved watching the two of them interact. It gave her hope that Marika's future was assured.

So she was shocked when she realized that the rose-shaped birthmark over Marika's heart seemed to be fading. At first she thought it must be her imagination, but the next day, after the baby's bath, it seemed even lighter. Her heart beating in her throat, she took a wash cloth and a dab of liquid cleanser and rubbed lightly on Marika's chest. Marika giggled as though she were being tickled, but Tianna wasn't in the mood for laughter. Because the "birthmark" was almost completely gone by the time she finished rubbing. All that was left was a splotch of brown, perhaps a birthmark in itself, but hardly shaped like a rose in any way.

Someone had drawn a rose shape on Marika's chest with permanent ink. And it had certainly fooled them all for long enough to help plant the seed that this baby was Garth's.

The prince knocked on the door of the nursery half an hour later for his daily visit. She let him in and immediately showed him what she'd found. He stared at the spot, then turned and looked into her eyes.

"Who would have done something like this?" he asked, and she knew right away that he was wondering about her.

Her heart dropped. Was he always going to suspect her now? If so, it was over. Because she couldn't live that way. And he shouldn't have to, either.

"I didn't do it," she told him evenly. "Whoever did do it obviously wanted you to think she was yours. And the only person doing suspicious things in that regard that I know of has been Janus."

"Janus." He grimaced, rejecting it out of hand. "That's crazy."

"Didn't you tell me he was an amateur artist? Who probably has permanent ink pens and the ability to draw a believable-looking rose?"

"But no motive." He shook his head, reaching to pull Marika's little shirt down and wrap her in her blanket so that he could lift her and take her with him. "The DNA results are due tomorrow. That ought to answer a lot of questions. Let's wait until then before we start blaming people."

That infuriated—and worried her. What was going to happen to Marika if it turned out she had no genetic ties to the Roseanovas? Everyone had been pretty clear. She would be going to the orphanage.

Tianna couldn't let that happen. But how could she stop it?

"Find Marika's mother," she muttered to herself, and suddenly she had another idea. Talking about Janus's artistic talent had reminded her that Garth had said he spent a lot of time at the artists' colony in Sedona. Since the man seemed to have a strange connection to this case, perhaps she should try calling some of the medical facilities there.

By the next morning, after some interesting phone calls, she did something even better—borrowed a car and headed down through the red rock canyons to Sedona herself. And in one doctor's office, she hit pay dirt.

"I know exactly who you're talking about," the office clerk told her, looking concerned. "Danielle Palavo. Yes, she was a patient of ours and I remember when she had that baby. Just a second, let me pull her file. I think we probably have a copy of the baby's birth certificate."

Tianna waited anxiously, and when the clerk came back and thrust the photocopy of the birth certificate across the counter at her, she did a double take. Baby Marika had been born in the local hospital to Danielle Palavo. And the father was listed as Garth Roseanova. Tianna caught her breath, feeling a little stunned.

"Did you ever see the baby's father?" she asked.

"I don't think so," the clerk said, wrinkling her nose. "There was an older man, tall and distinguished-looking, who sometimes came in with her. He always seemed so courtly and so concerned about her. But they never seemed like a couple to me. He was more like a father or an uncle or something like that. At least, that was the way it seemed to me."

"Janus," Tianna murmured, guessing but pretty sure she had it right. "Do you have Danielle's address?"

The clerk hesitated. "Well, we would have her old address, but I don't know if I should hand it out, you know. And…" She bit her lip and winced. "She died a little over a week ago. I guess you didn't know that?"

Tianna gripped the edge of the counter. "Died! Oh no."

The clerk nodded sadly. "Yes, she had a very weak heart and childbirth just about did the poor thing in, I'm afraid. And such a cute baby." She shook her head. "Doctor took it pretty hard. He'd known her since she was young, I guess."

Tianna steadied herself. "Can I talk to the doctor?"

"Sorry, he's out of town right now. But if you leave your name and number…"

Tianna drove back to Flagstaff in a daze. What would this do to Marika's future? Nothing good, she was afraid. But there still was the mystery of Janus's part in all this. And why the baby had ended up in the castle yard. Not to mention Garth's name being on the birth certificate.

Bridget had been watching Marika and she jumped up when Tianna came in.

"Oh, Miss…I mean, Your Highness, they're all waiting for you in the library."

The DNA results.

Thanking Bridget, she took a deep breath, kissed Marika and started out again.

The meeting didn't take long. The results were indisputable. Baby Marika's DNA showed no connection whatsoever to the Roseanova family. The full scientific report was read and they all sat quietly for a moment, mulling over the implications.

Tianna was numb. So much had been explained today, but there was still an awkward question. What was Marika's poor mother thinking, putting Garth on the birth certificate? It was all so incredibly sad.

One by one, the others rose and left, first Marco, then Princess Karina, then the doctor who had brought in the report. Prince Garth and Tianna were the only ones left, and they sat silently for a few moments.

"I guess I owe you an apology," she said at last.

He cocked an eyebrow and waited for her to explain.

"For thinking you were Marika's father, I mean," she said quickly. "For being such a pest about it."

His wide mouth quirked at the corners as he regarded her. "It was a perfectly natural mistake to make," he said.

Her gaze met his. Was he almost smiling? She was dying for a real smile from him, one that crinkled the corners of his eyes and lit his face with tenderness.

"You might be interested in this," she said. "I found Marika's mother."

Garth rose and came to the couch where she was sitting, sinking down beside her. "Really."

Quickly, she related what she'd found out in Sedona. He watched her steadily as she talked. He didn't seem very surprised, and when she finally paused for breath, he shook his head and said, "Poor baby. What a way to start her life out."

His first thought was for Marika and that warmed her. But when she said, "I think the tall man the clerk mentioned might be Janus," he nodded.

"It was."

She stared at him. "How do you know?"

"I had a long talk with Janus while you were gone."

"He's back?"

"Yes. And I caught him going into the nursery with his pens, obviously planning to touch up that phony birthmark."

"No!" She covered her mouth with her hands, her eyes huge. "So that was him, too!"

"Yes." He looked uncomfortable, his eyes haunted. "He crumpled before my eyes when I caught him. Emotionally. I'd never seen him like that before." He shook his head. "How can you be that close to someone for that long and yet not really know him?"

She reached out and took his hand. It felt so good to touch him again, but her purpose was purely comfort.

"But he told me about Danielle," the prince went on. "She used to work here, you know."

"No, I didn't know."

"Yes. She was an upstairs maid for a couple of years. I vaguely remember her. But according to Janus, she was a sweet and very vulnerable person and he sort of fell in love with her. He says she didn't ever think of him as anything but a friend," he added quickly. "And he is not the father of the baby. But she had no family and he took her under his wing and saw her often down in Sedona. He says she had a crush on me from the beginning and eventually wove a whole web of fantasy around a relationship she imagined between the two of us. When she got pregnant, she insisted I was the father, even though Janus knew that wasn't possible."

"Was she mentally ill?"

"I would say the evidence suggests she was, to some degree. At any rate, Janus loves Marika, but he knew he couldn't care for her himself. So he decided to see if he could manipulate us into adopting her into the family.''

She shook her head. ''Why didn't he just ask?''

''I wish I had a good answer for that, Princess Katianna.''

At the sound of Janus's voice, she jumped and turned to see the tall man coming into the room. He looked gaunt, broken, and her heart went out to him despite everything.

''I can only plead a sort of temporary insanity of my own,'' he continued, standing before them abjectly. ''My judgement has been sorely impaired for the last few weeks. And I have come to say goodbye.''

Tianna looked at Garth. He looked tense, a muscle working at his jaw, but he didn't say a word. She turned back to Janus.

''Tell me about the letter, the one naming the prince as her lover that fell out of Marika's clothes that first day,'' she said. ''Did she really write it?''

He nodded. ''That was only one of many letters that she wrote. She lived in a dream world much of the time toward the end.''

''Poor thing.''

''Yes. It was agony watching her slowly fade away. And I promised her I would make sure Garth took Marika and raised her in the family. Of course, that was a foolish thing to promise.'' He smiled gently at Tianna. ''Still, there were times I had some hope. When you arrived and took such a shine to the baby, I couldn't believe the luck of it. It couldn't have worked out better if I'd planned it. It all fell together, like some kind of destiny was at work."

He looked at her sadly. "I was a little bit crazy when I left the baby in the yard the way I did, not really sure what would happen, living in a kind of a fog. I was still mourning the death of Danielle, you know. It hit me particularly hard, I must admit. And then you came and picked the baby up. I saw you. I was watching from the window, keeping an eye on her. You picked her up and I knew right away that fate had stepped in. And once I realized who you were—well, it was all so perfect."

"You knew who I was?" Tianna asked in surprise.

"Of course. I keep up on these things."

"Why didn't you say something?" Prince Garth demanded.

Janus drew himself up in something very close to his usual fashion. "I would not presume to interfere, Your Highness."

"Oh," Garth said sarcastically. "Of course not. What was I thinking?"

Tianna grabbed his hand to quiet him. "Tell us more, Janus," she said. "I want to know all of it."

He explained how he had the idea to create the rose birthmark on top of the natural little mark Marika already had. And how he found the cloth from the old country to wrap her in. How he intervened to pretend the orphanage had chicken pox.

"I apologize," he said quite humbly. "Of course, I can never make up for what I've done. And it is impossible for me to stay in your employ. I'm leaving you my address in Sedona, in case you feel the need to get in touch with me or pursue some sort of legal action.''

''Don't be ridiculous, Janus,'' the prince said shortly. ''I don't want you to go.''

Janus didn't bend. ''I think it best, Your Highness. If upon reflection you decide you would still prefer me by your side, I will return with alacrity. But I think you should have some respite to think over all the ramifications of such an act. And in order to facilitate this I bid you adieu.''

Bowing, he left the room. Garth looked at Tianna. She looked at him. And despite everything, they both had to struggle to keep from laughing. The man was over-the-top with formality.

''Hush, he'll hear us,'' she said.

''He deserves to hear us. He deserves to be laughed at. The old bugger.''

''Oh, no, Garth. You have to have some compassion for him. He was only doing what he thought was best for Marika.''

''Compassion is dangerous,'' he told her gruffly. ''It makes you let things go you should take care of.''

Is that why you can't forgive me?

She didn't say the words out loud, but her eyes conveyed them. Instead of answering, he pulled her close and kissed her hard, trying to blot out that question. She melted in his arms, opening to him with a warm abandon that told him she would be his, if he would take her. Her arms slid around his neck and she arched beneath his hands. And he felt his system react, wanting her, needing her, aching to take possession of her body so that he could be sure he'd won her heart, touched her soul. He could love this woman, take her into his life forever. If only his demons would let him.

He pulled her close against his chest, cradling her in his arms, pressing her to his heart. Tears filled her eyes. She knew he was fighting a battle inside. He wanted her, and yet there was something in him that wanted him not to want her. She wished she knew which would win out.

"What about Marika?" she asked him, drawing back so that she could look into his handsome, beloved face. "Will she be going to the orphanage now?"

A storm came up quickly in his eyes, his face, and he rose from the couch without answering. She watched as he left the room and a hard fist of despair formed in her chest. If only she'd known the consequences of pretending to be someone she wasn't from the first.... If only.

Chapter Ten

"There are times when castles really seem like castles, and when a wedding is being held it's one of those times."

Tianna smiled when she overheard a middle-aged woman say this as she passed her group in the hallway. She pretty much agreed.

The castle was filled with people, most of whom she'd never seen before, although she had come across a cousin or two here and there and the reunion squeals had been deafening. The excitement was contagious. There was definitely something in the air.

Looking around the place, she could hardly believe they had been able to make such a transformation in such a short period of time. Huge bouquets of white carnations spilled out from every corner. White streamers were draped from the rafters. Bunches of white balloons made attractive backgrounds to sprays of greenery studded with white lilies. And here and there against the lacy magic of all the whiteness, long-stemmed red roses, a symbol of love, of the Roseano-vas, of the royal house itself.

The ceremony was to be performed outside, under an arched arbor decked with climbing red roses. Tables were set up all through the rose garden, each set with bone china and tall crystal champagne flutes. The centerpieces consisted of cages with white doves inside. The members of an orchestra were arriving and setting up in the area allotted for them, each dressed in white formal wear.

It was going to be a beautiful wedding, and Tianna was looking forward to it. But in some ways, she was dreading what would come after the ceremony was over and the last toast had been made. Her own personal deadline would come then. What was she going to do?

Her future hinged on what the prince decided to do about Marika. He'd once told her that the baby would go to the orphanage if she wasn't biologically his. Was that still his plan? He hadn't said anything different. She had to know. After agonizing for hours, she'd made her decision. She would adopt Marika herself, if she could find a way to do it. She had no legal standing. That was a problem. But she would do anything she could to keep that adorable baby from being dumped in the orphanage.

Whatever happened, she would be leaving soon after the wedding. It was high time she got back to Seattle and tried to pick up the pieces of her life and get on with it. Leaving Garth behind would be a wrenching experience, but staying here would be heartache as well. Besides, no one had asked her to stay.

She gave one last lingering glance to the garden and started back inside. It was time to begin getting ready. The ceremony was only a few hours away.

Tianna wished her mother could see her in the dress she was wearing as Princess Karina's Maid of Honor. It was very much the type of thing her mother liked, sort of prom dress meets wedding gown with a little Las Vegas thrown in. The bride was all in white lace and at first she'd wanted Tianna in white, too. Luckily, Tianna and Donna, Kari's friend who'd arrived to be a bridesmaid, were able to talk her out of it and the dress Tianna wore was a very pale sea-green instead. Donna was wearing a lighter shade in the same style.

The wedding itself was about half an hour away and Tianna was wandering in a side yard, waiting for her call, trying to avoid running into any more cousins. She especially hoped to avoid Cordelia, who, she'd heard, was searching for her in hopes they could have a nice long talk.

"No thanks, Cordelia," she muttered, turning the corner on a hedge and almost running into Crown Prince Marco.

"Oh!" she said, moving aside.

But he smiled, more friendly than he'd been lately. "You look very beautiful, Princess Katianna."

"Thank you Your Royal Highness." The truth was, she felt beautiful. The hairdresser had done wonders with her hair, with a little consulting help from Kari's friend, Donna, and it settled around her face in a frame of subtle ringlets that made her feel like something out of a medieval fairy tale. The dress fit perfectly, its long skirt swishing around her legs as she walked, its tight bodice showing off her form to advantage. "That is very kind."

"Call me Marco."

"Then you must call me Tianna."

"I will. Especially as I believe we are destined to be brother and sister very soon."

"You think so?" She looked doubtful and he took her arm, leading her to a wrought iron bench along the side and inviting her to sit beside him while they talked. From where they sat, they could hear the cooing of the doves and the various sounds of the orchestra musicians tuning up.

"Why do you doubt it?" he asked her.

She shrugged. "He resents me now. I don't think I can be married to someone who feels the way he does."

Marco looked into the distance, silent for a long moment. Then he turned back to her.

"I know Garth is a tough nut to crack," he said. "He won't be easy to live with, either. But I think you will find the effort to be worthwhile." He smiled at her. "You have to understand that in some ways, Garth was scarred more than any of us by what happened during the Escape, when our parents were killed."

She shook her head. "I'm afraid I really don't understand...." Her voice trailed off.

"Of course you don't. So I'll try to explain it to you." He settled back and narrowed his eyes as though picturing the past. "Garth was about eight or nine when it happened. He was an active child and he'd been befriended by our martial arts instructor. Hendrick cultivated Garth, took him hunting, taught him special moves, made him feel very important. So on the night of the Escape, when our section of the city was burning and we were hiding, preparing to be smuggled out of the country, he used that friendship to get Garth to let him into the storage area that was our hiding place." He shrugged. "Garth had no way of knowing Hendrick was with the rebels. And that is how our parents were killed."

"Oh no." She put a hand to her mouth. In her mind's eye, she could see a young Garth, see his eyes as he realized how he'd been betrayed, how his mistake had led to the betrayal of his parents. No child should have to bear such a burden. She wanted to jump up and run to Garth, to comfort him, to tell him it wasn't his fault. At this point, though, she wasn't sure he would accept any such sympathy from her. "How terrible," she whispered.

"I just wanted you to know that story so you might

understand some of the background for why it's hard to get Garth's full trust.'' Taking her hand in his, he raised it to his lips and brushed a kiss on her fingers. ''But once you do, I think you'll find you have a staunch defender in Garth, a partner whose allegiance will last a lifetime.''

Rising, he bowed and strode quickly away. Tianna stayed where she was and thought over what he'd told her. It did throw some light on why Garth acted the way he did. But she wasn't sure understanding his motives would do anything about changing his actions. Or his feelings.

The ceremony was beautiful. The music lifted it onto an ethereal plane. Princess Karina was stunningly lovely and Jack Santini, with his dark, Italian looks, was as handsome as the Roseanovas themselves.

Tianna was standing beside a radiant Kari and Garth was only a few feet away with Marco and Jack. Dressed in the Nabotavian military uniform, all in white with gold braid and epaulets, with a glittering array of medals on his chest, he looked breathtakingly handsome.

The minister was repeating the familiar words about love and commitment and forgiveness and Tianna's gaze met Garth's. She didn't shy away and neither did he. They might have been alone under the arbor. For a few minutes, they stared into each other's eyes and time stood still. Tianna could hardly breathe. It was as though a connection had been made between them, a mind meld, a bond that was too strong for either one of them to break, no matter how much he might wish to. All the longing she felt for him was there, all the sadness. All the love.

And then the spell was broken. She blinked and suddenly it was as though it had never happened. The ceremony was over, Jack was kissing Kari, and people were standing up to applaud. She took a deep breath. If only…

The next half hour was mostly confusion as people shouted greetings and reached across others to shake hands or grab her for a kiss. She laughed and kissed back and answered questions, but her mind was on Garth. Out of the corner of her eye, she always knew exactly where he was.

Bridget came out from the house carrying Marika, and Tianna turned to watch her in surprise. She made her way directly to Prince Garth, who reached out and took her as though he'd expected her. Curious, Tianna moved closer to the crowd around him, trying to hear what was being said.

"Her name is Marika," he was saying, smiling at Cordelia who was staring at him in shock. "After my mother."

The murmuring was subdued but only out of uncertainty.

"Prince Garth," a stout lady said firmly. "Are you telling us that this is your child?"

Tianna held her breath. Suddenly he looked out and met her gaze again.

"Yes," he said deliberately. "Marika is mine."

Tianna turned away. She was trembling and she wasn't sure if it was because she was so glad he'd done this, or because she was disappointed that her dream of adopting the baby herself was up in smoke. Someone spoke to her but she couldn't stop. Quickly she made her way out of the area. A moment later, she found herself striding down the driveway and she realized she was heading for the little gazebo where she'd first seen Garth. Could that really have only been a little over a week ago? It wasn't until she stepped into the little building that she felt she'd found a place she could be. She turned slowly, remembering the different person she'd been when she'd stopped here before.

Dropping to sit on the window seat, her skirt billowing out around her, she leaned against the backdrop and closed her eyes. She would be leaving soon. But at least Marika was taken care of. That was only right, and she was deeply relieved.

She opened her eyes again when she heard someone approaching. She wasn't really surprised that it was Garth. Her heart began to race like a locomotive. There was no help for it. Wherever he was her heart would be.

He stepped into the gazebo looking tall and handsome. "We've got to stop meeting here," he said softly, his eyes unreadable.

She smiled at him. "I don't think that will be a

problem," she said lightly. "I'll be leaving in a few hours."

His face didn't change and she went on, quickly. "I want to tell you how glad I am that you've accepted Marika as yours. I was prepared to ask if I might adopt her myself if you didn't do it."

"Really?" He gazed down at her steadily. "What happened to your career in photography?"

"I wouldn't have given that up, not entirely," she said.

"Good," he said firmly, his head to the side. "Because I'm hoping you will consider taking charge of documenting the return to Nabotavia. We're going to need an official photographer, you know. We don't have one as yet."

Her heart jumped at the thought. What an exciting job that would be! And she would get to be with the royal family, and with Marika…. But she shook her head. "I don't really see how I could do that," she admitted sadly.

"It wouldn't take up all your time," he told her, as though that was her main concern. "It would be a package deal, you know."

She frowned, wondering why she had the feeling there was a spark of amusement brewing in those eyes. "What are you talking about?"

"Well…" He shrugged casually. "Marika's going to need a mother."

Her heart skipped. "I suppose that would be best."

"I thought maybe you and I could go ahead and get married...."

Her breath caught in her throat, but she wasn't going to let him see her excitement. She pretended to frown at him. "Does this mean you're sort of hiring me on as a permanent nanny?"

The corners of his mouth twitched. "Actually, I was thinking of a more well-rounded role for you."

"Really?"

"Really." Reaching out, he took her hands and pulled her to her feet, then drew her in against him, his arms around her, his face against her hair. "I'm crazy about you, Tianna. You do realize that?"

She shook her head. Tears were filling her eyes. "No, you can't be."

"But I am." He tilted her face up and dropped a kiss on her lips. "I can't help it. It's just there. So don't forget to throw that in with your other equations."

She was almost afraid to hope, but he sounded so convinced—and convincing. "Garth, are you sure?" she asked, searching for the truth in his eyes.

"Watching you today during the ceremony, seeing the pure goodness and honesty that shines in your eyes, I realized what a fool I've been. It's taken me a few days to come to my senses." He kissed her lightly. "Can you forgive me?"

"I don't know," she said, laughing up at him. Her heart was so full. "Compassion can be dangerous. Or so you've advised me."

"I'm not asking for 'compassion,'" he said huskily as he nuzzled into her neck. "Plain old 'passion' will do quite nicely."

"That, sweet prince," she said as her body began to celebrate his touch, "you don't have to worry about."

He tasted her mouth and she clung to him, floating on happiness, but the sounds of yelling and crashes that had been growing in the background finally caught their attention and they both looked back up toward the castle, straining to see what was causing all the commotion.

"Oh no!" Tianna cried. "Look! The cows are out again. They're heading right for the reception!"

"Is that a fact?"

She looked up at Garth, surprised by his reaction. "Is Marika…?"

"Bridget took her back in."

"Oh, good." She sighed, then looked back up the hill.

Tables were overturning. Doves were fluttering free. People were yelling. But the three black and white cows marched relentlessly on, not seeming to notice the pandemonium they were creating.

Garth pursed his lips, but his eyes couldn't mask his amusement. "This always seems to happen when you let people set up events in the area between the livestock pens and the vegetable garden," he noted dryly.

Tianna shook her head. "We can't just stay here and let this go on."

"Can't we?" He pulled her close again. "I say, let the chaos commence. We have other things to concern ourselves with."

She looked up at him uncertainly. "But…"

"Hush," he said, pulling her down onto the window seat with him. "We have a lot of missed kissing time to make up for."

"Well, when you put it that way." She sighed happily as he curled his arms around her and began dropping tiny nibbles along her jaw line. "I think you've just given me an offer I can't refuse."

* * * * *

Next month, look for
Crown Prince Marco to meet his match in
COUNTERFEIT PRINCESS—the final
installment in Raye Morgan's captivating
CATCHING THE CROWN miniseries!

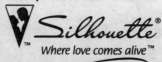

If you enjoyed what you just read,
then we've got an offer you can't resist!

Take 2 bestselling
love stories FREE!
Plus get a FREE surprise gift!

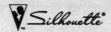

Coming soon from

SILHOUETTE *Romance*®

Teresa Southwick's

DESERT BRIDES

*In a sultry, exotic paradise,
three American women bring three handsome
sheiks to their knees to become...Desert Brides.*

July 2003
TO CATCH A SHEIK
SR #1674
Happily-ever-after sounded too good to be true to this
Prince Charming...until his new assistant arrived....

September 2003
TO KISS A SHEIK
SR #1686
There was more to his plain-Jane nanny than met the eye.
This single dad and prince was determined to find out what!

November 2003
TO WED A SHEIK
SR #1696
A nurse knew better than to fall for the hospital benefactor
and crown prince...didn't she?

Available at your favorite retail outlet.

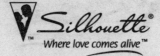

Silhouette®
Where love comes alive™

SILHOUETTE *Romance*®

COMING NEXT MONTH

#1672 COUNTERFEIT PRINCESS—Raye Morgan
Catching the Crown
When Crown Prince Marco Roseanova of Nabotavia discovered that
Texas beauty Shannon Harper was masquerading as his runaway fiancée,
he was furious—until he found himself falling for her. Still, regardless of
his feelings, Marco had to marry royalty. But was Shannon really an
impostor, or was there royal blood in her veins?

#1673 ONE BRIDE: BABY INCLUDED—Doreen Roberts
Impulsive, high-spirited Amy Richards stepped into George Bentley's
organized life like a whirlwind on a quiet morning—chaotic and uninvit-
ed. George didn't want romance in his orderly world, yet
after a few of this mom-to-be's fiery kisses…order be damned!

#1674 TO CATCH A SHEIK—Teresa Southwick
Desert Brides
Practical-minded Penelope Doyle didn't believe in fairy tales, and her
new boss, Sheik Rafiq Hassan, didn't believe in love. But their protests
were no guard against the smoldering glances and heart-stopping kisses
that tempted Penny to revise her thinking…and claim this prince as her
own.

#1675 YOUR MARRYING *HER?*—Angie Ray
Stop the wedding! Brad Rivers had always been Samantha Gillespie's
best friend, so she certainly wasn't going to let him marry a woman only
interested in his money! But was she ready to acknowledge the desire
she was feeling for her handsome "friend" and even—gulp!—propose
he marry *her* instead?

#1676 THE RIGHT TWIN FOR HIM—Julianna Morris
Was Patrick O'Rourke crazy? Maddie Jackson had sworn off romance
and marriage, so why, after one little kiss, did the confirmed bachelor
think she wanted to marry him? Still, beneath his I'm-not-the-marrying-
kind-of-guy attitude was a man who seemed perfect as a husband and
daddy.…

#1677 PRACTICE MAKES MR. PERFECT—
Patricia Mae White
Police Detective Brett Callahan thought he needed love lessons
to lure the woman of his dreams to the altar, so he convinced neighbor
Josie Matthews to play teacher. But none of his teachers had been as
sweet and seductive as Josie, and *none* of their lessons had evoked passion like this!

SRCNM0603